# THE REST ~~OF EARTH~~

## FOSSILS

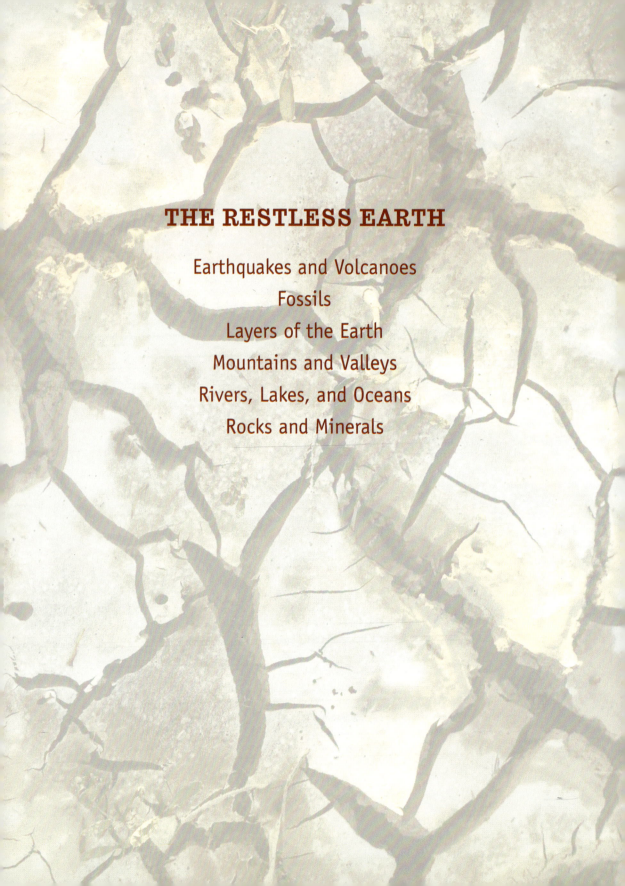

# THE RESTLESS EARTH

Earthquakes and Volcanoes
Fossils
Layers of the Earth
Mountains and Valleys
Rivers, Lakes, and Oceans
Rocks and Minerals

# THE RESTLESS EARTH

# FOSSILS

Gary Raham

THE FRANKLIN INSTITUTE

Chelsea House Publishers
An imprint of Infobase Publishing

# FOSSILS

Copyright © 2009 by Infobase Publishing

All rights reserved. No part of this book may be reproduced or utilized in any form or by any means, electronic or mechanical, including photocopying, recording, or by any information storage or retrieval systems, without permission in writing from the publisher. For information, contact:

Chelsea House
An imprint of Infobase Publishing
132 West 31st Street
New York NY 10001

**Library of Congress Cataloging-in-Publication Data**
Raham, Gary.
  Fossils / by Gary Raham.
    p. cm. — (Restless earth)
  Includes bibliographical references and index.
  ISBN 978-0-7910-9703-8 (hardcover)
 1.  Fossils—Juvenile literature.  I. Title.
  QE714.5.R34 2008
  560—dc22                  2008027077

Chelsea House books are available at special discounts when purchased in bulk quantities for businesses, associations, institutions, or sales promotions. Please call our Special Sales Department in New York at (212) 967-8800 or (800) 322-8755.

You can find Chelsea House on the World Wide Web at
http://www.chelseahouse.com

Text design by Erika K. Arroyo
Cover design by Ben Peterson

Printed in the United States of America

Bang EJB 10 9 8 7 6 5 4 3 2 1

This book is printed on acid-free paper.

All links and Web addresses were checked and verified to be correct at the time of publication. Because of the dynamic nature of the Web, some addresses and links may have changed since publication and may no longer be valid.

# Contents

▲▲▲

| | | |
|---|---|---|
| **1** | Fossils: From Natural Curiosities to Scientific Treasures | 7 |
| **2** | The Tortuous Road to Fossilhood | 22 |
| **3** | So Many Fossils, So Little Time | 38 |
| **4** | Marking Turning Points in Evolution | 50 |
| **5** | Finding and Excavating Fossils | 66 |
| **6** | Fossils in the Human Family | 78 |
| | Glossary | 91 |
| | Bibliography | 97 |
| | Further Reading | 101 |
| | Picture Credits | 104 |
| | Index | 105 |
| | About the Author | 111 |

# Fossils:
# FROM NATURAL CURIOSITIES TO SCIENTIFIC TREASURES

▲▲▲

*The tyrannosaur hurt. The breeze off the great water relieved the sun's heat, but her leg and side still ached where blood oozed from the gashes created by Three Horn's nose spike. She blinked her eyes, but the tattered fern fronds nearby failed to focus properly. Suddenly, the sky tilted alarmingly and one side of her body struck the cool earth. She found that she could not move. The familiar forest odors of pine resins and molding leaf litter settled about her as the world became silent and faded to black.*

MORE THAN 65 MILLION YEARS PASSED.

In the year 1992, a man named Charles Fickle took a walk with his dog through a half-built subdivision in Littleton, Colorado. He (or maybe his dog) found a large, rock-hard bone sticking out of the ground and suspected that it might be a **fossil**—the (usually) mineralized remains of a once-living creature. Fickle alerted the Denver Museum of Nature and Science. In response, the museum sent **paleontologists**—scientists who specialize in studying the remains of ancient plants and animals—to the site. They unearthed the entire right leg, ten teeth, a shoulder blade, and a tail vertebra, all belonging to the meat-eating dinosaur *Tyrannosaurus rex*. Fickle's dog did not get to chew on the bones, but Fickle got to chew on an unsettling thought: The world was once a vastly different place from what it is today.

What other fossil mysteries lie buried in the Earth awaiting discovery? Can these fragments of former lives serve as a lens through which prehistoric worlds come into focus again?

Ancient Romans would have called anything dug up from the ground a *fossilium*. That word became *fossile* in French, which came to refer, with a similar meaning, to everything from a miner's gold nugget to a burrowing crab. People often puzzled over peculiar "formed stones" that looked like giant or misshapen versions of familiar—or not so familiar—shells, bones, and animals. Naturalists eventually reserved the word fossil to describe such lifelike stones. Fossils are clues to old mysteries that demand explanations: When did this creature live? What did it look like when it lived? Why did it become extinct?

## FOSSILS, MYTHS, AND MONSTERS

Citizens of the classic civilizations of ancient Greece and Rome often answered such questions with myths and stories. The Greek city-states that nestled around the northeastern shores of the Mediterranean Sea roughly 2,500 years ago produced enough wealth to allow some of their citizens the time and means to travel within Greece, to Mediterranean islands, and to more distant lands where they encountered the fossilized bones of giant creatures.

Sometimes these fossils resembled smaller living species; but, sometimes, they appeared to be quite different. After Greeks had first seen living African elephants around 300 B.C., they correctly identified the bones of ice-age mastodons as oversized versions of elephants. Before that time, the hole in elephant skulls where the trunk attaches may have looked like a giant eye socket and given rise to legends about monstrous, one-eyed men called Cyclopes. Often, oversized bones were interpreted as the remains of heroes from Greek mythology and placed in temples or reburied with special ceremonies. These bones were found at sites where paleontologists continue to find the fossils of ancient mammals.

After the Greek and the Roman cultures that followed fell, the remnants of the Roman Empire formed a tight alliance with the Roman Catholic Church. Church beliefs became official state policy that was often brutally enforced to maintain civil order. Fossils became inconvenient objects not easily explained by narrow interpretations of church doctrine. They were described simply as remnants of Noah's flood, accidents of nature, or even as deliberate creations of a devil intent on confusing mere mortals.

## TONGUE STONES AND THE INSIGHTS OF NICOLAUS STENO

In the autumn of 1666, fishermen came upon a huge great white shark washed ashore on an Italian coastline. Perhaps because great whites can become "man eaters," they lashed the still-thrashing animal to a tree and killed it. The Grand Duke Ferdinando II in Florence, Italy, soon learned about the fishermen's adventure and ordered them to deliver the carcass to his palace. By that time, the shark's body was a bit ripe with decay, but the fishermen cut off the animal's head, loaded it on a cart, and sent it to the duke.

The duke respected knowledge and admired skilled and intelligent people. In fact, he had sheltered an astronomer named Galileo Galilei, who supported the then-radical idea proposed by Copernicus that the Earth orbited the sun and not vice versa after observing the satellites of planets with his newly invented telescope. In 1666, according to Alan Cutler, author of *The Seashell on the Mountaintop*, "Ferdinando's court was home to a scientific academy founded by several of Galileo's former pupils, determined to keep his spirit alive."

Even though the duke entertained many learned men at his academy, he chose Nicolaus Steno (1638–1686) to dissect the great white shark. Nicolaus, though only 28, had already made a

*(continued on page 12)*

## Griffins: Mythological Beasts or Dinosaurs?

From as early as 675 B.C., Greek travelers told tales of strange, lion-sized beasts called griffins that possessed huge, hooked beaks not unlike those of an eagle. They supposedly lived in the rugged desert country of central Asia near the Altai Mountains of what is now Mongolia. Adrienne Mayor, in her book *The First Fossil Hunters*, relates that Aelian, a learned compiler of facts and knowledge concerning natural history in the early A.D. third century, wrote, "The Bactrians say that griffins guard the gold of those parts, which they dig up and weave into their nests. . . ."

Griffins, Mayor contends, represent the first attempt to understand and reconstruct dinosaur fossils.

Griffins (left) are considered to be one of the first attempts by humans to understand dinosaur fossils—such as those of the *Protoceratops* (opposite page), the fossils of which were mistaken to be that of the mythological griffin.

The American paleontologist Roy Chapman Andrews (1884–1960) visited Mongolia in 1922 and found that the bony remains of dinosaurs were "strewn over the surface almost as thickly as stones." He and his team recovered more than 100 nearly complete skeletons of *Protoceratops* and *Psittacosaurus*, both of which display massive, beaked heads. *Protoceratops* has neck frills on a lion-sized body. Many white skeletons, partially eroded from the sides of red **sandstone** cliffs, stood out clearly in upright positions like eternal guards. Other skeletons lay on or near clutches of birdlike eggs, or close to the remains of young dinosaurs.

Flecks and chunks of gold erode from nearby mountains and sometimes wash into fossil-bearing sediments. Russian **archaeologists** once found the skeleton of a Bronze Age miner in the area whose leather bag still contained several gold nuggets. It is no wonder that ancient travelers who might have found this victim of the desert's heat and fierce storms might also believe that he was killed by living examples of the fierce-looking fossil creatures lying all around him.

*(continued from page 9)*

reputation for himself as a master anatomist—a person skilled at dissection and observation. By this time, he had already discovered the duct that carries saliva from the parotid gland to the mouth in humans—something that generations of physicians before him had failed to notice.

A crowd gathered to watch Steno begin his dissection. The sight of the dead shark with bulging eyes and jaws large enough to consume a person must have presented an amazing spectacle. Each jaw held 13 rows of teeth; the inner ones were soft and half buried in the animal's gums. Although the fishermen had cut some of the shark's teeth out for souvenirs, many of the teeth remained; the largest ones were perhaps 3 inches (7.6 centimeters) long. Steno realized immediately that the shark's teeth closely resembled objects known as "tongue stones." The mysterious tongue-shaped rocks were sold locally for their supposed medical and magical powers; since their origins were unknown, people thought that they grew inside the rocks in which they were found. Steno realized that the shark's teeth resembled tongue stones because they were one and the same thing—"as alike as one egg resembles another." Yet somehow the tongue stones had **petrified**, or turned to stone.

For many years naturalists and travelers explained away things like seashells on mountaintops. The Earth has "plastic forces" that just makes weird things, they said, or maybe the rain causes fossils to sprout like plants. But Steno and other careful observers saw that finding the assemblages of shells, shark teeth, and other marine creatures all together only made logical sense if these creatures had once been alive and living in an ocean—even if that ancient ocean bed had since risen to mountain heights.

Steno's contemporary in England, Robert Hooke (1635–1703), came to much the same conclusion a year later while looking at fossil seashells and petrified wood through his newly invented microscope. In his book *Micrographia*, which was written for the scientists of the recently formed Royal Society and

Fossils   13

The Grand Duke Ferdinando II in Florence, Italy chose Nicolaus Steno (*above*) to dissect a great white shark.

dedicated to King Charles II of England, he said, "That others of these Shells, according to the nature of the substances adjacent to them, have, by a long continuance in that posture, been petrify'd and turn'd into the nature of stone, just as I even now observ'd several sorts of wood to be."

The insights of Steno and Hooke—that fossils represented the remains of once-living creatures—began a revolutionary change in the way people viewed the world. If the forces of nature could transform ocean beds (and the creatures they contained) into stone while piling them up into mountains, then the Earth must have a history—a very long history. This concept ran contrary to orthodox Christian convictions of the time: that God had created nature all at once and pretty much "as is."

Steno's study of shark teeth led to many geological observations that he summarized in an essay for his patron, Grand Duke Ferdinando. "In various places," Steno wrote, "I have seen that the earth is composed of layers superimposed on each other at an angle to the horizon." Steno realized that, like the layers of pearl that form around a sand grain, those layers implied a history. The oldest layers must be on the bottom of the pile and the younger layers on top. This last statement summarizes what geologists now call Steno's **principle of superposition**.

"Water is the source of sediments," said Steno, and when water fills a container, whether that container is a glass or a vast basin, gravity ensures that the surface of the water is parallel to the horizon. As rocks and finer particles settle out, they will also come to lie horizontally. Steno's second principle, then, is the **principle of original horizontality**. If rock layers are tilted, that tilting must have happened after the sediments originally formed.

These were simple ideas, but not obvious ones. They made people realize that a fossil or any natural object contains clues to its own history. Steno's insights opened a vast new perspective on living things. The Earth transformed from a static stage for human activities into a restless, dynamic planet that not only changed the kinds of life it supported, but was changed by that life in turn. Fossils, the relics of ancient life, became the key to understanding Earth's long and exciting story, although it took time before everyone recognized their importance.

## SEA MONSTERS, FOSSIL HUNTERS, AND THE MYSTERY OF EXTINCTION

When 10-year-old Mary Anning's (1799–1847) father died in 1810 while hunting for fossils on the slippery cliffs of Lyme Regis on the east coast of Great Britain, she not only had to deal with the tragedy, but also find a way to help her poor family survive. Deborah Cadbury, in her book *Terrible Lizard*, says that the family had depended on her father's work as a carpenter to provide money, although they did make a few shillings selling "natural curiosities," like fossils, to tourists. One day, Mary found a beautiful snakestone—a fossil that today would be called an **ammonite**. (Its spiral shell reminded people of a coiled snake.) Mary ran through town showing off her discovery. A rich woman tourist offered her a crown for the find—a coin that could buy a week's worth of food. Mary realized that hunting for fossils along the rocky coastline could be both fun and profitable.

The next year, her brother Joseph found a huge, four-foot long skull eroding out of the cliff. The skull sported wicked-looking teeth like a crocodile, but had a pointed snout and large, round eye sockets almost like those of a bird. After a fierce storm the following year, Mary found the rest of the creature's body. All the bones were attached, although some were crushed. When townspeople helped her remove the slab of rock on which the fossil rested, they found that the creature measured 17 feet (5 meters) long. She sold that fossil (later named *Ichthyosaurus*, or "fish lizard") for enough money to feed her family for six months. Perhaps more importantly, she also attracted the attention of Reverend William Buckland (1784–1856), a student of the new science called **geology**.

Buckland was a rich gentleman, but he did not mind wading in the ocean or climbing cliffs with Mary. He said once that rocks "stared me in the face, they wooed me and caressed me, saying at every turn, Pray, Pray, be a geologist." In fact, he thought that geology was a "master sciencе . . . through which [he] could understand the signature of God." His position at Oxford University helped make Mary's discovery, and those of other English fossil

The *Ichthyosaurus* lived through two great extinctions but disappeared before the dinosaurs 66 million years ago. These shale fossils show an *Ichthyosaurus* mother with an infant and five unborn babies.

enthusiasts, more widely known. The man to impress in those days—Georges Cuvier (1769–1832)—was an ambitious French anatomist who lived in Paris and had a rich collection of fossils at his disposal in the Museum of Natural History there. He would later be called the father of modern paleontology.

After dissecting many animals in the course of his anatomical studies, Cuvier was convinced that fundamental laws govern the construction of animal anatomy just as the laws of force and motion discovered by Isaac Newton determine the motions of stars and planets. In other words, predators will always have teeth and claws designed for grappling with prey and strong, agile bodies to pursue them. Swimming animals will possess fins and streamlined bodies, even those creatures that look nothing like those living today—such as Mary Anning's bizarre fish lizard.

Cuvier and other fossil hunters of the time were aware of something else: Fossils did not appear randomly among the rocks. Older rocks contained a different collection of fossils than younger rocks and fossil creatures became progressively different in deeper (and thus older) layers of rock. Many of the fossils Cuvier found in what were called Tertiary rocks near Paris, for example, consisted of large mammals that often resembled living forms—much like the bones familiar to the ancient Greeks.

Mammoths and mastodons were similar to, but not the same as, African elephants.

Cuvier struggled to understand why these creatures no longer appeared to exist. He wanted to reconcile fossil discoveries with biblical accounts of Genesis. He reasoned that one of three things must have happened: (1) The animals must still be alive somewhere in the world; (2) the animals must have died off completely (become extinct) for some reason; (3) older versions of animals must have somehow changed over time to become the animals we see today. Cuvier favored option number 2. He decided that God must have destroyed old worlds in a series of disasters and then built new ones—a theory called **catastrophism**.

In fact, all of Cuvier's options are correct to some degree. Every now and then, animals once thought to be extinct are found in some remote location. In 1938, a species of fish thought to be extinct for 70 million years, the coelacanth, was found in an African fish market; a live specimen was later captured off the coast of the Comoro Islands. Such creatures are often referred to as **living fossils**.

In 1859, a scientist named **Charles Darwin** (1809–1882) convincingly showed in his book *The Origin of Species* that living things do change over time—or evolve—through a process he called **natural selection**. Darwin showed how living things with slight advantages can reproduce more effectively than other living things, and so their genes will be passed on. Over time—huge stretches of **geological time** that were becoming more and more evident to paleontologists—small differences become very large and noticeable.

## DINOSAUR MADNESS

English country doctor Gideon Mantell (1790–1859) and his wife Mary loved to hunt fossils. One summer day in 1822, Mary found a fossil resembling a mammal tooth in very ancient rocks that should not contain such fossils. Later, Mantell found teeth in a nearby quarry that looked most similar to the teeth of iguanas—tropical reptiles—except they were much bigger. Eventually, more

## Thomas Jefferson (1743–1826): American President and Paleontologist

In November 1796, Colonel John Stewart sent Thomas Jefferson three enormous claws that were discovered in a cave in western Virginia. Early the next year, in a letter to Benjamin Rush of the Philosophical Society, Jefferson wrote, "What are we to think of a creature whose claws were 8 inches long, when those of a lion are not 1 ½ inches . . .?" If perfectly created species were truly eternal, where were the living examples of these bizarre and monstrous beasts?

Jefferson thought he knew the answer: "In the present interior of our continent," he said, "there is surely space and range enough for elephants and lions."

In 1803, when he had been president of the United States for two years, Jefferson saw an opportunity to fund the exploration of western North America. Using $2,500 from Congress and some of his own money, he directed Captain Meriwether Lewis to find a trade route from the Missouri River to the mouth of the Columbia. Lewis enlisted his friend William Clark to share the command. While they prepared to get underway, Jefferson negotiated the Louisiana Purchase, giving the United States title to all the land between the Mississippi and the "Stony Mountains." The expedition produced an amazing record of the natural history and Native American cultures en route and laid the foundations of the **United States Geological Survey.**

Of those fossil specimens sent to him by Stewart in 1796, one species bears Jefferson's name: *Megalonyx Jeffersoni*, or "great claw." It was not a huge lion as he had first thought, but a ground sloth the size of an elephant. Sadly, it was no longer living in the unexplored western wilderness of America at the time of the Lewis and Clark expedition, but had vanished with the continental glaciers 10,000 years before.

complete skeletal discoveries showed that Mary had found the thumb spike of a giant reptile-like creature that was later named *Iguanodon* because of its similarities with living iguanas. Some twenty years later, paleontologist Richard Owen (1804–1892) coined the term *dinosaur* to describe a diverse group of mostly huge vertebrates (now called archosaurs) with many reptile-like characteristics. Dinosaur literally means "terrible" or "fearfully great" lizard, although dinosaurs are not lizards in the modern definition of the term.

Although first discovered in England (if we exclude the discoveries of ancient cultures), travelers and explorers in North America soon turned up new dinosaur finds. American scientist Joseph Leidy (1823–1891) at the University of Pennsylvania and Swarthmore College described early dinosaur finds starting in the 1850s and later, including the *Iguanodon*-like *Hadrosaurus*, which was found in Haddonfield, New Jersey.

Surveyors, railroad men, explorers, and scientists were turning up most new fossils in the deserts, plains, and mountainous country of the American West. Such discoveries excited not only scientists but the general population, too, with visions of gigantic beasts that lived long before humans walked the Earth. Mantell became obsessed with "the wreckage of former lives that had turned to stone" just beneath his feet.

## THE IMPORTANCE OF FOSSILS TODAY

Scientists continue to turn up amazing fossils. In 1994, the bones of *Sauroposeidon* were unearthed in southeastern Oklahoma—a dinosaur that weighed about 60 tons (54 metric tons) and stood 60 feet (18 meters) tall. In 2007, scientists studying a *Velociraptor* unearthed in Mongolia in 1998 (a predatory dinosaur that was portrayed in the movie *Jurassic Park*) found quill knobs on its forearm bone, a feature associated with the attachment of feathers. In 2007, researchers found a bee trapped in 10-to-15-million-year-old amber. The bee carried the pollinaria (pollen sacs) of the earliest known orchid species. In 2004, fossils discovered on the Indonesian island of Flores indicate that at least two species of humans may have coexisted just 18,000 years ago or less.

What kinds of questions can these and other fossil discoveries help scientists answer?

+ **Fossils help us know when things happened in the history of the Earth.** Scientists know that *Sauroposeidon* lived at a later time than *Apatosaurus*, for example, because it was found in sedimentary rocks that overlay the kind of rocks in which *Apatosaurus* was found—a fact that Steno would have appreciated.
+ *Fossils provide glimpses of some of the lost worlds of deep time.* Finds connecting insects to plants that they had pollinated provide valuable information about when certain ecological relationships between organisms evolved.
+ *Fossils document the major features of evolutionary change.* The discovery that a predatory dinosaur like *Velociraptor* possessed feathers lends support to the theory, based on anatomical and other evidence, that birds are the direct descendants of one branch of dinosaurs. (More traditional dinosaurs are now often referred to as "non-avian or non-bird dinosaurs.")
+ *Fossils provide clues to the reasons for extinctions—both normal and catastrophic kinds.* The kind and abundance of various fossils change dramatically at **extinction** boundaries. In fact, these changes define such boundaries. Fossils provide scientists with clues to understanding the mechanisms that cause major extinction events, which will provide guidelines to prevent human behaviors that might start or accelerate catastrophic extinction events today.
+ *Primate fossil remains provide insights into human evolution and reveal our intimate and necessary connections to the rest of the living world.* The ancient human species found on Flores stood only three feet tall. Human **evolution** on a small, isolated island resulted in the same kind of dwarfism demonstrated by other animals, like mammoths, that were isolated in a similar fashion. Fossil discoveries indicate that at various points over the last 2 million years, several human species

may have coexisted, although only *Homo sapiens* remains today. All the fossil evidence to date indicates that human beings have developed from preexisting species and depend on interactions with countless other living things in order to survive.

Because fossils are rare and because only some organisms are likely to become fossils, scientists must always use caution in drawing broad conclusions from studying fragmentary remains that are biased in favor of creatures with easily fossilized parts and that died under certain special conditions. The next chapter will demonstrate just how "lucky" a creature has to be to become an entry in the fossil record.

# The Tortuous Road to Fossilhood

▲▲▲

A MOUNTAIN LION KILLS A YOUNG DEER TO EAT AND PROVIDE FOOD for her cubs. Coyotes, ravens, and other scavengers eat their fill of the leftovers and scatter the bones. Microscopic organisms, mostly bacteria and fungi, break down living tissue into the atoms and molecules of which they are composed. These recycling processes, operating over Earth's entire 4.6-billion-year history, have ensured that life goes on. Carbon atoms that build the framework of a fat molecule in a person's big toe may once have nestled in muscle tissue in a *T. rex's* jaw. An oxygen atom from a protein molecule consumed in yesterday's hot dog may have passed through the lungs of Cleopatra. Fortunately, for anyone curious about the nature and evolution of past life on Earth, our planet does fail to recycle everything quickly in a straightforward way. Sometimes her restless forces make fossils.

## E(ROSION)-WORLDS AND D(EPOSITION)-WORLDS

Kirk Johnson, a **paleobotanist** at the Denver Museum of Nature and Science, likes to talk about D-Worlds and E-Worlds. In

E-Worlds like Colorado, where Johnson lives, wind and water expose fossils through **erosion**. Rivers rush down mountains, carving channels that expose rock that was once mud in some D-World long ago. D-Worlds, then, are low places like swamps and ocean beds where the sediments scoured from E-Worlds pile up and sometimes bury living things. **Deposition** rules in D-Worlds. To hide from the recycling powers of nature—such as wind, water, scavengers, and decomposers like bacteria—a living thing must enjoy a quick and long-undisturbed burial after it dies in a D-World in order to become a fossil.

Obviously, a lot of things get buried quickly and never become fossils. Countless worms live and die in the mud, yet almost none of these creatures fossilize because they do not have hard parts—things like bones, horns, shells, and teeth. Soft tissues of plants and animals *can* absorb or be replaced by minerals to become the "formed stones" that have so long intrigued people, but fossils are not always hard and mineralized. A fossil consists of the remains or traces left behind by a living creature. Some remains get preserved for a very long time with little alteration.

## MUMMIES, "SAPSICLES," AND TAR PIT DIVERS

In September 1991, hikers found the head and shoulders of a man melting out of a glacier high in the Alps on Italy's border with Austria. Five other bodies had been found that year to join six that were discovered between 1952 and 1990. Most of these corpses belonged to hikers or skiers who had made bad decisions or were surprised by a sudden storm. Most of them had died within the past few years or decades. But the so-called "Iceman," found in 1991, had met his end on some spring or summer day 5,300 years before. The ice preserved his clothes, tools, the pollen from hornbeam blossoms that floated in the air around him, and even traces of his last meal.

High mountain glaciers, like the one where the "Iceman" was found, act like refrigerators to preserve the remains of living things. Low temperatures keep bacteria and other decomposers

# 24 FOSSILS

A 10,000-year-old, 4-foot Siberian baby mammoth carcass is examined in the Arctic city of Salekhard in July 2007—a discovery that could help us understand more about climate change.

from performing their recycling chores. Because we are living during a warm interlude between a series of ice ages or glaciations extending back some 2 million years, the bodies of mammoths or other extinct creatures also become exposed as the glacier ice melts.

The word **mummy** may conjure images of a bandage-wrapped body chasing some archaeologist down a passage in an Egyptian tomb. Ancient Egyptians and other peoples have, in fact, intentionally removed internal organs and applied salt and other chemicals to inhibit decay in human bodies as part of their religious and cultural traditions. Scientists do not usually consider mummified human bodies to be fossils, but natural mummification does occur in both dry and cold climates to both humans and other animals. Three species of giant ground sloth, for example, lived in North America 13,000 years ago. The largest species, *Paramylodon*, could rear up 6 feet (1.82 meters) and weighed 3,500 pounds (1,590 kilograms). This veggie eater spent time in caves—perhaps seeking sheltered space when giving birth. Individual sloths also died in caves. Scientists have found complete sloth skeletons with hair, skin, nails, and soft tissues like muscles and tendons dried but still intact. Some sloth skin still contains small nodules of bone called ossicles, which are common in reptiles, but only found in armadillos among today's living mammals.

Insects, lizards, small mammals, and various plants and plant parts sometimes blunder into and get stuck in the gooey **resin** of certain trees. The resin, over long stretches of time, heat, and pressure, becomes **amber**. As fans of *Jurassic Park* movies know, amber can preserve **DNA (deoxyribonucleic acid)** and other complex organic molecules for millions of years. While reconstructing individual animals (like dinosaurs) from fragmentary bits of DNA is currently impossible, creatures trapped in amber provide a wealth of detail about the world in which they lived. For example, the husband and wife scientific team of George Poinar Jr. and Roberta Poinar have looked at a stingless bee trapped in amber with "gossamer wings outstretched and perfectly preserved down to the last hair" and contemplated what its eyes saw in a Dominican Republic rainforest 40 million years ago. By observing and recording hundreds of amber "sapsicles," they have convincingly recreated this animal's lost world in their book *The Amber Forest*.

A young Columbian mammoth searching for food 20,000 years ago steps on what he thinks is solid ground only to sink into the black goo of a **tar pit**—a natural pool of asphalt formed when organic material slowly decays as it heats up underground. He struggles, but only gets stuck more deeply. His cries attract dire wolves, perhaps an old saber-toothed cat, and giant birds of prey, called teratorns. Some of them get stuck in the tar as well, and what looked like a "free lunch" becomes their last meal. Scientists have "read" this and many similar stories while

Amber can preserve DNA and other complex organic molecules for millions of years, providing lots of detail about the world in which the organism embedded in the amber lived. Above, insects more than 38 million years old are embedded in two pieces of amber.

mining the famous La Brea tar pit traps in the center of Los Angeles, California. Many insects, birds, turtles, and plant parts also found their way into the tar. Quick burial and low oxygen preserved their remains intact—in this case for tens of thousands of years.

## CARBONIZATION: FOSSIL "ROAD KILL"

A paleontologist visiting Douglas Pass, Colorado, high in the Rocky Mountains, may use her rock hammer to pop apart a thick slab of **shale** and find the dark brown image of a *Macginitiea* (sycamore) leaf or a fossil cranefly. A musty smell reminds her of fish and rotting vegetation on a lakeshore. The leaf or the insect has been **carbonized**: partially decayed, wrapped in slime, crushed, and heated.

Herbert W. Meyer, a paleontologist with the U.S. National Park Service, has studied this process in some detail at famous fossil beds (the site of ancient lakes) near Florissant, Colorado. The layers of shale at Florissant and Douglas Pass, as well as other locations in Utah and Wyoming, alternate with the ash from volcanic eruptions. Many of the early workers at these sites assumed that animals and plants in the lakes died and were preserved in mass dying events during volcanic eruptions, but careful studies have shown that much of this preservation happened in the periods between these violent events. "The thin shale layers formed slowly over many decades," says Meyer, "whereas the layers of **volcanic ash** accumulated much more rapidly."

Images taken of Florissant fossils with a **scanning electron microscope** have shown that leaves and delicate insect wings are covered with a thin layer of billions of tiny plant cells called diatoms. Growing abundantly in lake water enriched with silica from volcanic ash, these diatoms and bacteria covered dead insects, fish, and leaves floating on or in the lake with a thin film that is almost like plastic wrap. This film helped preserve the organisms long enough to be buried by successive layers of **silt** and volcanic ash. The weight of these layers ultimately

# 28 FOSSILS

A 50-million-year-old Eocene Age fish fossil *(Priscacaraliops)* was found at the Green River Formation near Kemmerer, Wyoming.

compressed and heated the remains until they became dark carbon "ghosts" of the original animal or plant. These carbon films often display rich patterns and fine detail, although sometimes they do look more like ancient road kill.

## ON BECOMING A ROCK
Visitors to Arizona's Petrified Forest see what most people think of when they think of fossils: once-living things literally turned

to stone. Scientists rarely use the term *petrification* anymore. Instead, they speak of **permineralization** and **replacement**—processes that result in the conversion of living tissues to minerals

This petrified tree trunk in Yellowstone National Park in Wyoming was transformed into its current state by volcanic activity in the area.

like **quartz** (silicon dioxide, $SiO_2$), **calcite** (calcium carbonate, $CaCO_3$), or pyrite ($FeS_2$).

Imagine a huge pine tree, say an *Araucarioxylon* tree like those in Arizona's Petrified Forest, undercut and swept away in a flash flood. It ultimately drifts into a wide meander of the river where sand and muck bury it. Without the oxygen that bacteria and other decomposers need in order to feed, most of the tree's wood remains intact. Over a period of time, mineral-laden

## The Sternbergs Find a Dino-mummy

Though it does not happen often, fossil hunting can become a family business. Such was the case for Charles Sternberg and his sons Charlie, George, and Levi. In 1908, they had just collected a *Triceratops* skull in Wyoming, but were short on food and supplies. Just as Charles and Charlie got the wagon hitched and ready to take into Lusk (the nearest town, 65 miles away), George found some interesting bones sticking out of a high ridge of sandstone. George and young Levi, who was fourteen at the time, decided to stay and work on the new fossil rather than risk not finding it again. Charles and Charlie left to get food.

George and Levi worked hard for five days until their family returned, surviving on a few old potatoes that they boiled a few at a time. As they uncovered the fossil from the rock, they got more and more excited. They knew they had found something special. Finally, George lifted a huge slab of sandstone off the chest of the fossil animal and stared in wonder. "I realized that here for the first time, a skeleton of a dinosaur had been discovered wrapped in its own skin," he wrote later. The Sternbergs had found a dinosaur that had water filters through the tree's muddy tomb, entering pores and even the empty spaces within individual plant cells, whose walls are made of relatively tough materials like cellulose and lignin. As water evaporates, minerals crystallize out of solution. This process is called permineralization. Replacement occurs when the carbon compounds making up the tough lignin and cellulose of the wood are later replaced by calcite, iron, or other mineral compounds.

first dried out and become a natural mummy—perhaps because it died in some protected place where no predators could reach it—and then was transported to a final resting place during a flash flood that quickly buried it. In this final tomb, it was petrified and preserved for more than 65 million years.

George and Levi Sternberg found this mummified carcass of an *Edmontosaurus* dinosaur in Niobrara County, Wyoming in 1908.

A collector can section a completely mineralized piece of wood with a rock saw and see even microscopic cellular detail. Bones have a similar porous structure that makes them perfect for permineralization. The phosphate compounds that make up bone may change composition somewhat by incorporating chlorine and/or fluorine atoms rather than being completely replaced. Iron sulfides may replace calcium carbonate shells or other organic materials buried in low-oxygen, ocean-bottom mud, in a process aided by bacteria, to produce fool's gold, or pyrite. Such fossils truly look like creatures dipped in gold.

## CASTS, MOLDS, AND OTHER VARIATIONS ON THE THEME

Not all fossils become exact replicas of their living model. In the tree example, the sand and mud around the trunk may have hardened to stone, but all the organic material of the tree ultimately decayed completely. This left a hollow cylinder, or **mold**, that displayed the exact shape and outer detail of the tree trunk. If this natural mold then filled with minerals or more mud before breaking apart or eroding away, a **cast** of the tree would remain behind. The cast would have the shape and outer texture of the tree but inside it could be pure **agate**, a form of silicon dioxide. This kind of petrified fossil is also called a **pseudomorph**, or "false form."

Shells also make good fossils because they are hard and resistant to change. Animals create their shells out of a form of calcium carbonate called **aragonite**. Aragonite often recrystallizes into the more stable form of calcium carbonate called calcite. At other times, shells end up as casts or molds or both.

Some popular fossils called trilobites are the casts, molds, and petrified remains of arthropods whose shells were composed of chitin, like modern crabs and insects. A person finding a mold of a trilobite shell can easily make a cast of the animal by pressing some clay into the mold. Because trilobites and other arthropods grow larger by shedding old shells and growing new ones after their bodies take up water and expand, each animal has the

# The Tortuous Road to Fossilhood 33

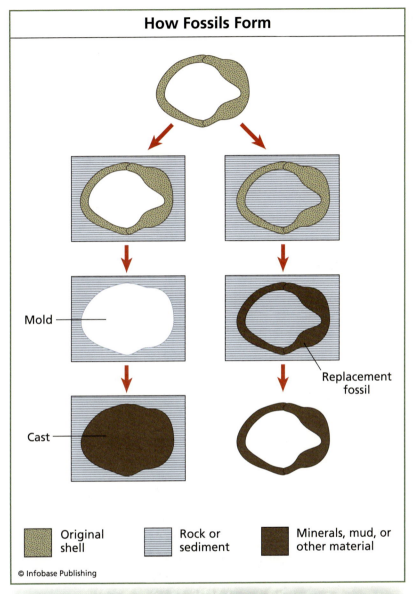

This diagram illustrates mold and cast formation, two ways that fossils develop.

potential of leaving multiple fossils if conditions encourage fossilization. Fossils of shed skins are an example of a special kind of fossil called a **trace fossil**—a remnant left behind by a living thing.

## TRACE FOSSILS: TRACKS, DUNG, AND MORE . . .

Tourists at a beach leave thousands of tracks in wet sand, but most of these footprints are washed away by the tide or covered over by other wandering tourists. Now and then, the sun's heat hardens tracks in soft mud before successive layers of sand and dirt bury and preserve them. Many dinosaur tracks formed in this way along ancient seashores that bordered a seaway that once separated North America into two landmasses a hundred million years ago. A number of these tracks were discovered in sandstone in Morrison, Colorado, just west of Denver. A volunteer group called the Friends of Dinosaur Ridge preserves them and shows them to many visitors every year.

But sometimes, scientists do not find typical footprints. Instead, they may find footprint casts. Here is how these casts form: A footprint made in mud hardens, and then wet sand fills the track depression. As the water of the seaway ebbs and flows, many alternating layers of mud and sand will cover the prints. Over long periods of time, the mud gets compressed to **mudstone** by the weight of overlying sediments. Similarly, sand becomes transformed into a harder rock called sandstone. Unless protected in some way, mudstone will erode away first leaving sandstone casts of the original footprints.

Perhaps the biggest exposed dinosaur trackway in North America parallels the Purgatoire River in southern Colorado. In a remote spot that has been part of a military testing range for many years, a slab of resistant sandstone 100 yards (90 meters) long and about the width of a two-lane highway stretches away into the distance. A photo in the January 1993 issue of *National Geographic* magazine captured dinosaur track expert Martin Lockley examining prints produced by five giant **sauropods** that had walked side by side. Each footprint was about as wide as the end of a telephone pole. Visitors to the site can also see the three-toed tracks of predators—perhaps *Allosaurus*-type **theropod** dinosaurs. Such trackways reveal secrets about the size,

The Tortuous Road to Fossilhood 35

Dinosaur tracks found in Picketwire Canyon in Animas County, Colorado.

weight, travel speed, behavior, and ecological relationships of these extinct creatures.

Even fossilized dung (or droppings), called **coprolites** by paleontologists, provide valuable clues about an animal's diet and environment. Scientists have found fragments of bone, teeth, fish scales, mollusks, wood, leaves, seeds, and even footprints (usually of micelike early mammals) in coprolites. Distinctive burrows in plant-eating dinosaur coprolites show that dung beetles, not unlike those alive today, helped recycle those wastes. Other vertebrate trace fossils include eggs and the nests that sheltered them. These reveal how certain dinosaurs and lizards reproduced and cared for their young. Intact

## The Scoop on Some King-sized Poop

Members of the Royal Saskatchewan Museum in Canada found the largest currently known fossil coprolite in 1995 in sediments from the end of the age of dinosaurs. The fossil measured about 17 x 6 x 5 inches (44 x 16 x 13 centimeters) and contained chunks of bone belonging to an animal about the size of a modern cow. The microscopic distribution of bone fibers and blood vessel arrangement in the ingested bones implies that they had belonged to a juvenile dinosaur. Because of the coprolite's size (probably 2.5 quarts [2.3 liters] when fresh) and the age of the sediments, this jumbo trace fossil probably belonged to a *Tyrannosaurus rex*. (In fact, the scientists found the coprolite while taking a break from a *T. rex* excavation just 1.25 miles [2 km] away.) Members of the science team also recovered scattered remains of a *Triceratops* nearby. Young *Triceratops* calves may well have been part of a well-balanced *T. rex* diet.

embryos in some eggs provide clues about rates of development and which eggs belong to which adults.

What kind of trace fossils have humans left behind? What products of modern technology will best survive the trials and tribulations of becoming a trace fossil? Only time—and lots of it—will tell for sure, but scientists suspect that objects like glass soda bottles and plastic forks will survive a very long time. Hopefully, a paleontologist in some future E-World will not conclude that we worshipped Barbie dolls and tiled our houses with cafeteria trays.

# So Many Fossils, So Little Time

▲▲▲

A CHINESE PROVERB SAYS, "A PICTURE'S MEANING CAN EXPRESS TEN thousand words." In 1787, geologist James Hutton (1726-1797) saw a geological feature much like the one shown on the opposite page. That feature, consisting of two rock layers lying at sharp angles to each other and separated by an eroded surface, is known in geological terms as an **angular unconformity**. It inspired Hutton to write two massive books (*Theory of the Earth*, volumes 1 & 2). He was justified in exceeding the Chinese proverb's expectations, because the image of the rocks revealed something profound: that the world was a *very* old place. Fossils implied the same thing, but not always so graphically all in one place.

Nearly 200 years later, the writer John McPhee struggled, as all of us must, to understand the vast stretches of time demonstrated by Earth's layered **topography**. He coined the term *deep time* as a label. He states in his book *Basin and Range*, "Numbers do not seem to work well with regard to deep time. Any number above a couple of thousand years—fifty thousand, fifty million—will with nearly equal effect awe the imagination to the point of paralysis."

The image deserves a closer look.

So Many Fossils, So Little Time 39

Above is an example of angular unconformity at the Olympic Coast in the state of Washington, with sharply dipping vertical rock layers deposited during the Miocene Era underneath horizontally bedded gravel deposited during the Pleistocene Era.

## UNCONFORMITIES: GLIMPSES OF DEEP TIME

The figure above shows a gash that exposes the rocks under the ground at the Olympic Coast in Washington State. The lowest set of layered rocks lie *vertical* to the ones above them. When the lower rocks were formed in some ancient sea, they must have lain horizontally—for as long as it takes to deposit sediments that thick. (Remember Steno's principle of original horizontality.)

Then, some process of uplift pushed the rocks to a vertical position. We know today that mountains rise roughly at the same speed that fingernails grow. Erosion must have created the jumbled rocks between the two-layered sequences. That, too, took a lot of time. Then, the sea either advanced or the land sank (**subsided**) and the long process of creating many new layers began. The sea retreated again (or the land rose) and more erosion took place to form the soils of Washington.

Before Hutton's time, the history of our planet consisted of "a short tale of uninterrupted erosion," in the words of the late paleontologist Stephen Jay Gould. Hutton realized that angular unconformities showed clearly that Earth's history involved long periods of alternating episodes of deposition, **uplift**, and erosion. The uplift part of the process implied that powerful regenerative forces created mountains from old seafloors that, in turn, eroded away to form new, layered deposits on some fresh ocean basin. Hutton thought this process to be never-ending. He saw "no vestige of a beginning—no prospect of an end." Later scientists would find this phrase a bit imprecise, but Hutton had produced a major geological insight from a striking image of Earth's forces frozen in time.

## THE PRESENT AS THE KEY TO THE PAST: UNIFORMITARIANISM

Charles Lyell (1797–1875) was born the year Hutton died, but geologists usually link his name and Hutton's because he wrote an influential book, *The Principles of Geology* (published in three volumes from 1830 to 1833), promoting the essence of Hutton's ideas. Lyell emphasized the concept that forces in the past must have acted essentially as they do today. This concept acquired the name **Uniformitarianism**. Lyell denied the existence of biblical-style floods like those proposed by Cuvier, yet the fossil record does show that entire ecologies changed abruptly on rare occasions. Geologists have since learned that Earth has endured volcanic eruptions, weather changes, ocean currents, and even hits by space rocks (**meteorites**) far more severe than anything humans have witnessed during recorded history. Nevertheless, Uniformitarianism rightly emphasizes that most geological history proceeds by the forces of erosion, sedimentation, and uplift that we see today. He estimated the age of some of the oldest fossil-bearing rocks at the then-unheard-of age of 240 million years.

Charles Darwin also liked Lyell's old-age estimate for fossil-bearing rocks because it provided more time for living things to evolve according to his mechanism of natural selection. Darwin and Lyell became good friends. Lyell strongly supported Darwin's *The Origin of Species* when it was published in 1859. He even extended the concept of evolution to human beings, something that Darwin was not prepared to do at the time.

## THE MAP THAT CHANGED THE WORLD

William Smith (1769–1839) dug ditches and lots of them. He surveyed the English countryside as part of major canal construction projects in the late eighteenth and early nineteenth centuries. Canals served transportation needs then the way interstate highways do now. Smith's father, a blacksmith, died when he was eight. Smith could not afford an education beyond grammar school. But he worked hard, performed his job well, and kept his eyes—and his mind—open.

His work as a surveyor took him into coal mines where he could see the distinct layers, or **strata**, of the Earth clearly. Many of these strata held fossils. As he traveled the length and breadth of England on various jobs, he recognized something that no one had truly noticed before: Certain fossils *always* appeared in particular strata no matter where he went in the country. As Simon Winchester relates in his book, *The Map That Changed the World*, this realization struck him clearly on the cold evening of Tuesday, January 5, 1796. He had decided not to return home that night because the weather was too bad. As he sat at a table at the Swan Inn in Dunkerton, he scribbled an excited note with one phrase underlined for emphasis: "Fossils have long been studied as great curiosities, collected with great pains, treasured with great care and at a great expense, and showed and admired with as much pleasure as a child's rattle or a hobby-horse is shown and admired by himself and his playfellows, because it is pretty; and this has been done by thousands who have never paid the least regard to that wonderful order and regularity with which Nature has disposed of these singular productions, and assigned to each class its particular stratum."

Smith became obsessed with an idea: He would create a map that would show in complete detail the inner structure of England. In essence, it would be a geological road map that would reveal details like those that had so impressed Hutton. Smith's project would take nearly twenty years to complete. It would cost him dearly both in money and good health. But in the end, he created an enormous 8-foot-by-6-foot (2.4 m by 1.8 m) detailed, full-color map that would change the way people thought about the world. He provided a book whose layered pages of rock and stone contained "letters" of distinctive fossils that spoke about past times and vast mineral and energy treasures to those who could read them. And although his map only outlined the geological "innards" of England, other scientists found the same layers—and some of the same fossils—all over the world. Fossils especially useful for marking distinct points in geological time are called **index fossils**.

## WHAT MAKES A GOOD INDEX FOSSIL?

Index fossils should: (1) be easy to find, but unique to particular layers of rock; and (2) change gradually over time with a well-defined sequence of forms. The shells of various invertebrate animals often make good index fossils because they belong to relatively small creatures that reproduce in large numbers, fossilize readily, and possess ridges, pores, spines, and other distinctive markings. Some examples include ammonites and baculites: squidlike mollusks that floated in ancient seas and preyed on fish, clams, worms, and trilobites. Ammonites possessed coiled shells and baculites created straight shells not unlike skinny ice cream cones. Horseshoe crablike creatures called trilobites also make good index fossils. In some of the oldest oceans, small trilobites floated near the surface of the water, larger species swam actively (probably preying on microscopic organisms), and other species crawled and dug in the ocean-bottom ooze. Clams like *Inoceramus* and shelled creatures called brachiopods that held on to rocks and other objects with short stalks can be added to the list, along with various corals and sponges. The United States Geological Survey (USGS) shows some of the index fossils used to identify points in geological time on their Web site.

All the creatures mentioned above live in oceans and are **macroscopic**—visible with the naked eye. Some of the best index fossils are **microscopic**—only visible with magnification. Scientists can find (if they know where to look) lots of microscopic forms that come from both watery and **terrestrial** environments. Once plants invaded the land, they produced spores, and later pollen, in vast quantities. The shapes and surface patterns of spores and pollen grains are very species-specific. Paleontologists can infer a lot about the ecology of terrestrial habitats from spores and pollen that fell into lakes, bogs, or swamps.

Ocean **microfossils** that are useful as index fossils include the following:

*Conodonts*: Teethlike structures in very old rocks. In 1983, conodonts were found to be body parts of soft-bodied animals not unlike modern lancelets (related to primitive fish).
*Foraminifera* (or "forams" for short): Tiny animals with shells that existed from 300 million years ago to the present.
*Ostracods*: Small crustaceans related to water fleas.
*Coccoliths*: Calcareous plates found on certain algae.
*Graptolites*: Colonial animals that lived in ancient oceans.

Index fossils serve as great aids to scientists in determining the order of events and species in the geological record. They thus help mark what paleontologists refer to as **relative time**. But

# 44 FOSSILS

These shells are rich with calcium and were constructed by single-celled marine animals called *foraminifera*. The shells have pores through which the animals could extend their pseudopodia (or "false feet") in order to catch food. Deposits of *foraminifera* like these are the key component of limestone.

could fossils—or anything else—help provide concrete numbers with which to mark points in deep time, even if those numbers might be unimaginably large? Such numbers could provide an **absolute time scale**.

## JUST HOW OLD ARE YOU, MOTHER EARTH?
Various people had observed that as you travel deeper into mines, the temperature goes up. Many people thought that perhaps the Earth burned like a glowing cinder, gradually cooling off after a fiery birth. It seemed reasonable to physicists in the nineteenth

century that they might be able to determine the age of the Earth if they could figure out how long it would take for a planet-sized blob of matter to cool down from a completely **molten** state.

The right man for this task appeared to be a Scottish math teacher's son named William Thompson (1824–1907), who later became Baron Kelvin of Largs, or Lord Kelvin for short. Lord Kelvin became a university freshman in 1834 when he was 10 and had written his first mathematical paper by the age of 17. By the time his career was over, he had written 500 scientific papers, had invented electrical meters and navigation aids, and had helped create the transatlantic cable between the United States and Great Britain. In other words, the man had credentials.

Lord Kelvin did some math. He made a few general assumptions about the melting temperature of rock and whether some heat energy might come from other chemical reactions as the Earth cooled. He knew his figures were somewhat rough, but overall he decided the Earth could not be much older than 100 million years. He also figured the Earth would have been cool enough for living things to evolve for perhaps 20 to 25 million years. That is a long time, but was it long enough for the processes of evolution described by Darwin and supported by Lyell and other scientists of the day? Could the great Lord Kelvin be wrong? Could something else be keeping the Earth warm over much longer stretches of time?

In 1898, Marie (1867–1934) and Pierre Curie (1859–1906) discovered radium and polonium in pitchblende, an ore of **uranium**. These new elements gave off unusual amounts of energy in the form of **X-rays** and subatomic particles, which Marie called **radioactivity**. Later, in 1903, Pierre Curie and Albert Laborde found that radium gave off significant amounts of heat.

Ernest Rutherford (1871–1937) did further studies on radium and confirmed its heat-generating properties. In a 1905 article in *Harper's Magazine* he wrote, "In the course of a year, one pound of radium would emit as much heat as that obtained from the combustion of one hundred pounds of the best coal, but at the end of that time the radium would apparently be unchanged and would itself give out heat at the old rate." Eventually, the amount of heat given off would slowly decrease, but Rutherford calculated that the pound of radium could keep giving off heat at about the same rate for a thousand years.

Rutherford knew that uranium ores were so common that the heat generated by radioactivity could account for much of the heat

## Don't Wake Up Lord Kelvin!

Joe D. Burchfield relates in his book *Lord Kelvin and the Age of the Earth* that Rutherford had a chance to announce his conclusions about the heat-generating powers of radioactive elements in 1904 at the Royal Institution in England. He knew that his discoveries would mean a revision in the age of the Earth. Lord Kelvin was an old man at that time, but still carried considerable prestige among scientists, and so Rutherford became a bit anxious when he found out that Lord Kelvin would be in the audience. He described the experience this way some time later:

> I came into the room, which was half dark, and presently spotted Lord Kelvin in the audience and realized that I was in for trouble at the last part of the speech dealing with the age of the earth, where my views conflicted with his. To my relief, Kelvin fell fast asleep, but as I came to the important point, I saw the old bird sit up, open an eye and cock a baleful glance at me! Then a sudden inspiration came, and I said Lord Kelvin had limited the age of the earth, provided no new source of heat was discovered. That prophetic utterance refers to what we are now considering tonight, radium! Behold! The old boy beamed upon me.

generated by our entire planet. This also meant that Lord Kelvin's calculations were way off the mark because radioactivity would have kept the Earth's interior hot and toasty for a very long time. Not only that, the emission of subatomic particles by decaying radioactive elements occurs in such a regular fashion that it can be used as a kind of slow-ticking clock—just the kind needed to keep track of old Mother Earth's age. Also, temperature, pressure, and chemical reactions do not affect these "**atomic clocks**."

The bad news about radioactive elements is that you have to look in **igneous rocks**, like those found in volcanoes, to find them rather than in the **sedimentary rocks** that hold fossils. However, layers of igneous rocks often bracket layers of fossil-bearing rocks, so you can determine minimum and maximum ages for various fossils. By dating the oldest rocks found on Earth and by dating meteorites that were formed at about the same time as the Earth, scientists ultimately pegged her age at 4.6 billion years.

## THE MODERN GEOLOGICAL TIME SCALE

The modern geological time line shows Earth's entire history as recorded in rocks. This timeline has been pieced together since William Smith's day by overlapping sections from all over the world. **Eons** are the longest blocks of time, followed by **eras**, **periods**, and **epochs**. The **Phanerozoic Eon** covers the span of time in which you can see fossils of one sort or another with the naked eye. It begins 542 million years ago with an error of 1 million years in either direction (this is indicated by the + and − symbols next to each number; the error comes from uncertainties in the dating techniques used). Evidence of microscopic life in rocks extends back 4 billion years to the beginning of the **Archean Eon**. For the most part, paleontologists study fossils from the three eras of the Phanerozoic: The **Paleozoic Era** (age of old life), **Mesozoic Era** (age of middle life), and **Cenozoic Era** (age of recent life).

## 48 FOSSILS

| Millions of years ago | Eons | Eras | Periods |
|---|---|---|---|
| 0 | Phanerozoic | Cenozoic | Neogene |
| 65.5 | | | Paleogene |
| 100 | | Mesozoic | Cretaceous |
| 150 | | | Jurassic |
| 200 | | | |
| 250 | | | Triassic |
| 300 | | Paleozoic | Permian |
| 350 | | | Carboniferous |
| 400 | | | Devonian |
| 450 | | | Silurian |
| 500 | | | Ordovician |
| 542 | | | Cambrian |
| 630 | Proterozoic | Neoproterozoic | Ediacaran |
| 850 | | | Cryogenian |
| 1,000 | | | Tonian |
| 1,200 | | Mesoproterozoic | Stenian |
| 1,400 | | | Ectasian |
| 1,600 | | | Calymmian |
| 1,800 | | Paleoproterozoic | Stratherian |
| 2,050 | | | Orosinan |
| 2,300 | | | Rhyaeian |
| 2,500 | | | Siderian |

© Infobase Publishing

This diagram shows the progression of geological time over millions of years. Boundaries between time periods often represent major extinction events.

Paleontologists (and geologists) memorize eras and periods early in their careers. They often use a mnemonic device like the following to remember the periods of the Phanerozoic:

**C**old **O**ysters **S**eldom **D**evelop **M**any **P**recious **P**earls.
**T**heir **J**uices **C**ongeal **T**oo **Q**uickly.

You just never know what will get some people's memories going.

# Marking Turning Points in Evolution

▲▲▲

THE EARTH CREATES ONLY A MISERLY HANDFUL OF FOSSILS—OFTEN ALL that remains is a creature's mineralized framework of bone or shell. But every now and then paleontologists discover rich deposits of fossils in such great numbers or that are so well preserved that an instant of deep time flickers into view in great detail. Such rich seams of fossil life help paleontologists flag the geological time scale with significant events in the history of life, just as humans mark birthdays, graduations, and marriages during their own much shorter lifetimes. This chapter will note some spectacular fossil sites, look at a few in more depth, and highlight some of life's major evolutionary achievements on the long road from microorganisms to mankind.

## HUMANIZING THE GEOLOGICAL TIME SCALE

If the geological timeline shown at the end of Chapter 3 seems like just a list of weird names and big numbers, it can be made more real by using the human body to illustrate. Stretch out your arms and let the middle finger of your left hand represent Earth's

# Marking Turning Points in Evolution 51

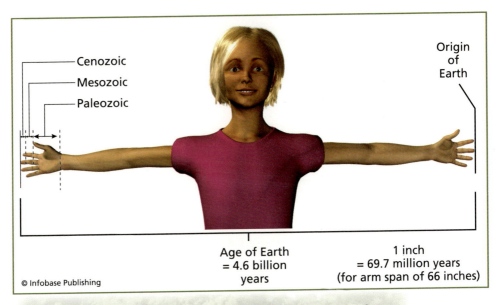

The geological timeline can be illustrated using the armspan of an average student.

origin and the middle finger of your right hand represent the present moment. One arm span now equals 4,600 million years. If that arm span is, say, 66 inches, then 1 inch = 69.7 million years. The first fossil animals big enough to see with the naked eye show up in sediments 540 million years old—about to the wrist of your right hand. The Paleozoic Era, or "age of old life," extends from your right wrist to the base of your right fingers. The basal and middle finger joints of the right middle finger represent the entire "age of middle life" (the Mesozoic Era, which most people associate with dinosaurs) and the last finger joint, including the fingernail, represents the "age of new life" (dominated by mammals), or the Cenozoic Era.

Filing that fingernail down would erase all traces of our species, *Homo sapiens*.

The divisions between major periods and eras reflect changes in the fossil record. The most drastic changes happened at the boundaries between Paleozoic, Mesozoic, and Cenozoic Eras. Fossils show that 90% of Paleozoic species disappeared 251 million years ago between the Permian and Triassic Periods and 65% died 65 million years ago between the Cretaceous and Tertiary Periods. (Remember all that **C**old **O**ysters **C**ongeal **Q**uickly stuff at the end of Chapter 3? The Tertiary is the first period at the beginning of the Cenozoic Era.) Paleontologists study these **mass extinction events** carefully, hoping to understand them so that *Homo sapiens* can avoid turning up on a list of extinction fatalities.

## PRECAMBRIAN ETERNITIES

So what was going on during that long stretch from when the Earth was congealing from hot star stuff just beyond your left fingertip to your right wrist? Life existed during much of that **Precambrian** time, but it was microscopic. Sometimes, it left little more than chemical traces in ancient rocks until about 3,500 million years ago. Then, some chains of simple plant cells—informally referred to as pond scum—coiled together into some amazing pillars of cells and sand called **stromatolites**. Fossil stromatolites look a bit like giant concrete stalks of cauliflower, but they changed the course of history forever by evolving the process of photosynthesis—a technique for using light energy to turn water and carbon dioxide into sugars with the aid of a "helper" molecule called chlorophyll. Stromatolites, as a result, had to "pass a little gas." Unlike the methane that escapes from animals from time to time, plants release oxygen—the waste product of photosynthesis.

The earliest living cells made energy by breaking the chemical bonds in methane and various sulfur compounds. Oxygen, because it reacts with vital chemicals very quickly, was a deadly poison. Stromatolites were so successful that they drove the first living cells to "hellish" places like hot sulfur springs (like those in Yellowstone National Park) and deep-sea hydrothermal vents

## Marking Turning Points in Evolution 53

Stromatolites are the oldest life form that still exists today. The oldest stromatolite fossils are thought to be around 3.5 billion years old. These stromatolites are found in Shark Bay in western Australia.

where hot magma from Earth's interior sizzles out of cracks on ocean floors. Various species of such primitive **Archaea** live near these vents today.

Stromatolites passed lots of gas—for hundreds of millions of years. Ocean water absorbed all it could, but then oxygen leaked into the air. After more hundreds of millions of years, many rocks literally rusted, forming what geologists call **banded iron formations**. The sky gradually changed colors, too, from the vomit green of a methane and ammonia atmosphere to the familiar blue, oxygen-nitrogen mix we see today.

## THE GARDEN OF EDIACARA

Toward the end of the **Proterozoic Eon** (lower right forearm on our human timeline—roughly 630 million years ago), living things began forming colonies of cells that resembled transparent air mattresses. Geologist Reg Sprigg first found evidence of these creatures, called **Ediacarans,** in the Flinders Ranges of southern Australia in the 1940s. A schoolboy by the name of Roger Mason found another Ediacaran in an English quarry in the late 1950s. Scientists later discovered similar fossils in the ancient rocks of Russia, Canada, and Namibia. The Ediacarans display various shapes, but they seem to have no front and rear ends. These "gutless wonders" may have survived by exchanging nutrients and wastes with seawater and perhaps forming symbiotic associations with cells that could photosynthesize.

About 100 million years later, another revolution took place—one that banished stromatolites to far corners of our modern world like Shark Bay, Australia, and wiped out the Ediacarans. Predators brought their jaws and other weapons into the food chain. The evolution of new forms slipped into a higher gear and began the Paleozoic Era (which covers, in our time line, the palm of your right hand). Let us examine some firsts in the history of life and see where to find the fossils that reveal the once-lost worlds of prehistory.

## THE PALEOZOIC: SHELLS, CREEPY CRAWLERS, AND MONSTER FISH

The first shellfish, including trilobites and brachiopods, evolved in diverse communities containing corals and the ancestors of every major group of modern creatures. The first simple plants invaded the land and were followed quickly by the first land-loving arthropods. Perhaps 40 or 50 million years later, the first **tetrapods** (four-legged vertebrate animals) came ashore. Late in the Paleozoic, lush first forests composed of **lycopods** and other primitive plants sheltered a wealth of amphibians, reptiles, and giant insects.

## Important Fossil Sites

The western cape of South Africa has produced important marine fossils. Fossils from Rynie, Scotland, show us what some of the first land plants and animals looked like. Coal beds near a tributary of the Illinois River close to Chicago yield fantastic plant and animal life from some of Earth's first forests. From the tops of mountains in the Canadian Rockies, paleontologists have uncovered a rich record of some of our planet's first animals.

## The Strange Beasties of the Burgess Shale

In the late summer of 1909, Charles Doolittle Walcott (1850–1927), then the secretary of the Smithsonian Institution in Washington, D.C., found an amazing collection of creatures from the earliest Paleozoic high in the Canadian Rockies. The dark shales in which he hunted had once been oxygen-starved sand on a Cambrian seafloor at the foot of a deep trench. His field notebook shows drawings of a creature (*Marrella*) that he informally called a "lace crab," along with sketches of other arthropods with armored body segments and head shields. Predators apparently swam in the ocean world these animals inhabited, forcing them to develop defenses that made them look like tiny, crawling fortresses. Walcott, accompanied by his family and various students, returned to the Canadian Rockies and hunted fossils in the **Burgess Shale** for many summer field seasons. He ultimately collected more than 65,000 specimens of a shallow water community that was entombed in a landslide some 530 million years ago.

Walcott's discoveries showed the early Cambrian to be a time of rapid experimentation in body forms and survival strategies

## The Predator Found in Pieces

Charles Doolittle Walcott found many species in the Burgess Shale, most of which were new to science. He discovered something that looked like the rear end of a shrimp and was given the name *Anomalocaris* by its first discoverer in 1892, and something that looked like a pineapple ring. Walcott named this latter fossil *Peytoia*. Walcott thought *Peytoia* might have been some sort of primitive jellyfish. A third fossil, named *Laggania*, resembled a sea cucumber (a starfish relative) that had been smashed like roadkill. It had a roughly circular mouth surrounded by a ring of plates. All these fossils became part of Walcott's collection at the Smithsonian.

Some seventy years later, three researchers began looking at the Burgess Shale fossils in more detail and made some amazing discoveries. In 1978, Simon Conway Morris studied a specimen of *Laggania* and found an example of *Peytoia* about where Walcott had described an "indistinct mouth." In 1979, Derek Briggs realized, after studying hundreds of fossils, that *Anomalocaris* was not an entire animal at all, but some leg or other body part. Finally, in 1981, H.G. Whittington decided to risk damaging a large, indistinct example of *Laggania*, by taking it slowly apart to better see some partly hidden structures.

# Marking Turning Points in Evolution 57

that is now often referred to as the **Cambrian Explosion**. Virtually every major group of animals alive today has ancestors dating back to this time, including the **chordates**, the group from which vertebrates like humans developed. But the Burgess Shale also holds the remains of weird beasts that did not make the final cut—animals like *Opabinia*, with five eyes and a claw on the end of a "nose hose"; and *Hallucigenia*, a creature that was so strange, scientists did not figure out for a long time which end

When he did so, he found that his fossil represented the remains of a relatively large predator (about two feet long) whose mouth was the creature first called *Peytoia* and whose two feeding arms were the fossils called *Anomalocaris*!

In science, the name that counts is the name given to the first fossil discovered. *Anomalocaris* thus became the name of one of the first predators in the fossil record—a segmented terror whose shadow hung over the trilobites and other shellfish whose armor and spines were sometimes inadequate defense when it got hungry. Stephen Jay Gould reveals additional details in his 1989 book, *Wonderful Life*.

*Anomalocaris*

© Infobase Publishing

The *Anomalocaris canadensis* is an extinct animal thought to be related to modern arthropods.

was "up." Walcott found bits and pieces of the major predator of the day, a floating nightmare with tentacles and rotary teeth called *Anomalocaris*, whose appearance (and identity) also did not become clear until much later.

## THE MESOZOIC: DINOSAURS RULE, MAMMALS SQUEAK, AND FLOWERS START A REVOLUTION

Primitive mammals and dinosaurs evolved relatively early in the Mesozoic. The first birds, descendants of small, active, theropod dinosaurs, evolved sometime in the Jurassic. Flowering plants first appeared in the Late Cretaceous and out-competed other seed plants for dominance after an end-Cretaceous disaster.

## Important Fossil Sites

Thousands of small, early dinosaurs died at what is now called Ghost Ranch, New Mexico, a site that reveals a glimpse of life as it was there more than 200 million years ago. Fine-grained limestones in Germany continue to produce highly detailed fossils of plants and animals from marine and land habitats. Limestones from Araripe Basin, Brazil yield fossil plants and insects, some amazing fish fossils, and, most recently, crocodiles, turtles, dinosaurs, and spectacular **pterosaurs** (flying reptiles). But much of what we know about dinosaurs has come from the great American West.

## Dinosaurs of the Morrison Formation

Dinosaurs roamed vast stretches of what is now the North American West 150 million years ago. Much of the land on which they lived has since turned to rock. Layers of rock that are recognized as being similar over large areas are called **formations**. An Upper Jurassic formation called the **Morrison Formation** covers an area of 0.6 million square miles (1.5 million square km), bounded by central New Mexico in the south and the Canadian provinces of southern Saskatchewan and Alberta to north, and from central Kansas to the east and eastern Idaho to the west. Sauropod giants like *Apatosaurus*, *Diplodocus*, and the common, so-called "Jurassic cow," *Camarosaurus*, wandered along waterways that often cut across semiarid country that was not too unlike an African savanna. Ferns and other plants took the place of grass, which had not evolved yet. The dominant predator, *Allosaurus*, 40 feet (12 m) long and armed with 70 curved teeth and ferocious toe claws, probably hunted in packs to bring down sauropod calves, stegosaurs, and other veggie eaters.

Fossils from the Morrison Formation also include **conifers**, ferns, **cycads** (trees with trunks like pineapple skin and fernlike tops), and other important plants of that time, along with many animals including crayfish, insects, clams, lizards, pterosaurs, crocodiles, and frogs. Our distant mammalian cousins also turn up in great numbers. A site in Como Bluffs, Wyoming, has produced many rodentlike early mammals.

In 1909, paleontologist Earl Douglass (1862–1931) set out for northeastern Utah to find a dinosaur "as big as a barn" for Andrew Carnegie, a wealthy man who wanted to create an impressive museum exhibit. Douglass succeeded by finding an amazing site that eventually yielded (after 15 years of work) the remains of more than a dozen species of dinosaurs, including one of the most well-known, *Apatosaurus* (formerly known as *Brontosaurus*). But Douglass wanted to do more than dig up dinosaurs: He wanted to share the wonder of what he had found. He wrote in his diary, "I hope that the Government, for the benefit of science and the people, will uncover a large area, leave the bones and skeletons in relief and house them in. It would make one of the most astounding and instructive sights imaginable."

The U.S. government adopted his idea. The site is now called Dinosaur National Monument, located near Vernal, Utah.

# Schoolteachers Help Fuel the "Dinosaur Wars"

Douglass was not the first one to find the *Apatosaurus*. That honor fell to schoolteacher Arthur Lakes (1844–1917), who discovered some huge bones in sediments near Morrison, Colorado—the location from which the Morrison Formation gets its name. Shortly afterward, teacher O.W. Lucas found large bones in similar sediments near Canon City, Colorado.

Lakes first sent his specimens to a paleontologist at Yale: Othniel Charles Marsh (1831–1899), who was famous, in part, for his work in uncovering **hadrosaurs** in Kansas. Lucas sent his fossils to Edward Drinker Cope (1840–1897), another paleontologist famous for finding the first horned dinosaurs (a relative of *Triceratops*). Lakes also sent some bones to Cope because Marsh was slow in acknowledging his first letter and fossil shipment. Cope later had to give these bones to Marsh when Marsh hired Lakes to work for him.

Cope and Marsh had initially started out as friends early in their careers, but personal and professional differences between them grew. Finding the biggest and best dinosaurs turned into aggressive competition for both of them. When two railroad workers found the rich Como Bluffs site near Medicine Bow, Wyoming, Marsh hired them to excavate the site. (Lakes also helped with some of the early work.) Cope later sent men into the same area and the two crews eventually got into fights that even resulted in the destruction of some bones by one party so the others could not have them.

Marsh and Cope feuded from then on until Cope died in 1897. Marsh only outlived Cope by two years. Although Cope and Marsh described 135 species of dinosaurs between them, their behavior did not live up to the standards that scientists expect from fellow professionals.

## THE CENOZOIC: MAMMALS (AND FLOWERS) RULE

The Cenozoic saw the rise of all the major mammal groups, including horses, whales, monkeys, apes, and human beings. Flowering plants (also called **angiosperms**)—well, they flowered! Grasses became an increasingly important part of ecosystems. The Cenozoic began as a warm world that gradually cooled to produce a series of ice ages separated by minor warm spells lasting a few millennia. Human beings are living in such a warm spell now.

## Important Fossil Sites

A site near Darmstadt, Germany, more than 50 million years old, yields early mammals, birds, insects, and other creatures that lived in or near a lake in a semitropical area. Along Baltic Sea shores in Poland, Germany, and Denmark, amber (fossilized tree sap) contains flowers and plant parts, insects, and other arthropods. The Rancho La Brea Tar Pits (11,000 to 38,000 years old) in the center of Los Angeles, California, have trapped mammoths, dire wolves, saber-toothed cats, and a host of other animals in the goo of natural asphalt. In the Rocky Mountains of the American West, fantastic tropical animals emerge from today's oil shales.

## Cenozoic Eden: The Green River Formation

About the time the last dinosaur died, the Rocky Mountains in the middle of North America began their slow climb skyward. After 20 million years had passed, water drained from the highlands all around to create a series of lakes in what is now western Colorado, eastern Utah, and southwestern Wyoming. Forests of palms, alders, sycamores, and chestnut trees sheltered bats, collie-sized horses, lemurlike primates, clouds of insects, horned and tusked *Uintatheres*, and seven-foot-tall predatory ground birds. Lake Uinta at times covered 24,000 square miles (62,000 square kilometers)—bigger than Michigan's Great Lakes—and existed for 17 million years, leaving lake deposits 7,000 feet thick in places. In 1856, Dr. John Evans collected and described the first fossil

This group of fossilized fish was found in the Green River Formation in Wyoming.

fish from Green River sediments in the western United States. Dinosaur bone hunter Edward Drinker Cope also collected extensively in the area and published an important paper on fossil fish in 1871.

Today, anyone visiting a "rock shop" or nature store will likely find Green River fish fossils. Paleontologists (and amateur fossil hunters) continue to hunt the fossils of fish, freshwater stingrays, and rare birds near Kemmerer, Wyoming. Spots in western Colorado yield fossil insects and leaves. In 2002, volunteers helped the Denver Museum of Nature and Science, Utah State Parks, and the U.S. Bureau of Land Management personnel excavate more than 300 square feet (28 square meters) of **Green River Formation** leaf and insect fossils to line the walls of a new museum in Vernal, Utah. The work also discovered new specimens to illustrate the Parachute Creek Atlas Project—an Eocene fossil plant record that complements work done on "flashier" vertebrate species.

## MASS EXTINCTIONS: LIFE ON THE EDGE OF DISASTER

The fossils associated with the Paleozoic, Mesozoic, and Cenozoic Eras stand out by their differences. Paleontologists can see those dramatic differences in the rock. The boundary between the Mesozoic and Cenozoic Eras—the marker for the end of the reign of dinosaurs—is a seam of clay that can be covered by the width of a human hand. In the late 1970s, geochemist Lewis Alvarez and his father, Walter, a geologist and geophysicist, collected samples from the boundary layer exposed near Gubbio, Italy, where it is sandwiched between layers of pink limestone. They found that the layer contained a very high concentration of **iridium**, an element usually rare on Earth, but common in meteors and asteroids—the leftover debris of planet building during the birth of the solar system. Also present were deformed particles of quartz called **shocked quartz** that result from the impacts of meteors with the Earth.

Other scientists found these same features at sites all over the world. Radiometric studies dated the layer to 65.5 million years old—precisely the age of the Cretaceous-Tertiary boundary (abbreviated as the **KT boundary**) as determined by other methods. Alvarez calculated that an object the size of Mount Everest must have struck the Earth to leave a worldwide trace of this magnitude. That would have left a crater some 110 miles (180 km) wide. No one was aware of a crater that size until the early 1990s, when geologists found magnetic anomalies deep beneath northern Mexico. Further studies revealed a buried impact crater of the right size for such a collision. Walter Alvarez describes many of the details in his book *T. rex and the Crater of Doom*.

When it strikes, an object that size vaporizes itself and its target with enough force to put tons of debris into Earth's orbit. The "dirt ring" blocks sunlight and causes green plants and the animals that depend on them to die. Flaming rocks falling back to Earth cause massive, worldwide fires. The blast itself kills directly and creates huge ocean waves, or tsunamis.

But the evidence for mass extinction at extinction boundaries sometimes comes from fields of study other than geology. For example, paleontologist Peter Ward has spent much of his career studying the worst mass extinction of all time—the one at the boundary between the Paleozoic and Mesozoic. A 60-foot-thick layer of mudstone separating hundreds of feet of limestone marks this layer, which is located not far from Luning, Nevada. "The limestones above and the limestones below are packed with life," he says in his book *Under a Green Sky*. "What a supreme difference those two worlds show with clearly almost no survivors of some catastrophe grabbing the river of life and giving it a 90-degree kink into a whole new assemblage. . . ."

The culprit for this end-Permian extinction and many others, Ward believes, is rapid and severe climate change. Earth has many mechanisms for maintaining climate balance, but sometimes the scales tip wildly. Long and extensive volcanic eruptions much greater than anything seen in human history may sometimes shift the balance. Such events happened both at this boundary and during the KT event. The volcanoes poured vast amounts of carbon dioxide and sulfur dioxide into the air. Carbon dioxide acts like a thermal blanket, warming the Earth while sulfur dioxide forms sulfuric acid when dissolved in rainwater. The Earth's climate also changes more slowly as continental landmasses shift positions and ocean currents change. Long-term variations in the Earth's orbit and tilt relative to the sun also contribute to alternating periods of heat and cold.

During the last several hundred years, human activities have entered the mix of destabilizing events. Carbon dioxide levels have soared just since the 1950s, mostly from burning fossil fuels. Some scientists believe that by 2050, we could see carbon dioxide levels close to what they were during the warm tropical days of the Eocene that created the Green River Formation. Ward says he wrote his book to serve as a warning to heed the evidence of past climate change and its effect on extinction. "I'm scared . . .," he says, "and I'm not going to be silent anymore."

Knowledge of the deep past can help us plan for and make a better future.

# Finding and Excavating Fossils

▲▲▲

POPPING OPEN A ROCK TO REVEAL THE FOSSILIZED REMAINS OF another living thing can forge an electrifying connection to the deep past. The surprise and wonder of field discovery adds an element of treasure hunting that often makes paleontology an addictive career or pastime. Nevertheless, fossil hunting is hard work. But where prison convicts are forced to smash rocks under a blazing sun as punishment, paleontologists do it for fun—for limited grant money or teacher's pay. Paleo volunteers labor for free, excited by what they might discover in the next layer of rock. Fossils only form under special conditions, but those conditions occur often enough that fossils are not especially hard to find. A person simply needs to know how to find those places where nature or humans have uncovered long undisturbed burial grounds that have been compressed and hardened into stone.

## DISCOVERING E-WORLDS RICH WITH FOSSILS

Wind and water erode rock. Humans often help nature along. A budding paleontologist may find his or her first fossil by accident when a backhoe turns ground for a new subdivision or ball field.

Suddenly, the appearance of shells from an ancient sea or giant bones may jolt the finder out of his or her present to contemplate a long and mysterious past. Still, while luck plays a role, finding fossils with regularity and confidence requires a more systematic approach.

Geologists create color-coded maps that show exposed rock layers along with information about rivers, roads, and the topography, or "lay of the land." Fossil hunters can find these **geological maps** produced by the U. S. Geological Survey through the USGS Web site or at local stores catering to hunters, hikers, and climbers. (Maps are also available through state geological surveys.) In all cases, the ages of rocks are color-coded, so, for example, areas with Mesozoic rocks are shown in various shades of green, Cenozoic rocks are yellow, and Paleozoic rocks are purples, blues, and oranges. Curving **contour lines** give the height of the land above sea level. When the lines are drawn close together, it means the elevation changes quickly, which may indicate ridges and valleys where erosion may have exposed fossils. Geological maps also contain information about rock orientation, as well as regional gravitational and magnetic forces that might be helpful in planning roads, railroads, and finding important mineral deposits.

Learning to read maps, use compasses, and search for possible fossil-bearing sites can be more fun when done as a group project. Many larger communities host rock or geology clubs or amateur paleontology groups. National organizations include the American Federation of Mineralogical Societies (AFMS), which has various regional subgroups. Visiting their Web site will lead you to more local organizations. Some of the paleontology groups open to amateur participation often partner with museums. The Western Interior Paleontological Association (WIPS) works with scientists from the Denver Museum of Nature and Science, for example, and the Paleontological Research Institution (PRI) can be reached through the Museum of the Earth, which is based in Ithaca, New York.

Members of local clubs often lead field trips to road cuts, quarries, mines, riverbeds, seashores, and other areas where

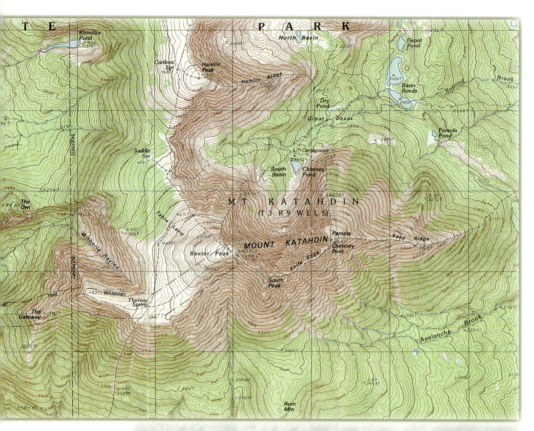

This topographical map shows the highest peak in the eastern United States, called Mt. Katahdin, in Baxter State Park, Maine. The lines indicate changes in elevation.

they can hunt on public land legally or on private land with permission. Various state and federal laws determine the kind of fossils that can be hunted on public lands and the techniques that can be used. For example, the surface collecting of invertebrate fossils may be allowed, whereas hunting and excavating vertebrate bones is nearly always restricted to professionals with special permits. It is important to know and obey these laws and get any required permission when hunting on private land.

Club membership may spark a lifelong interest in fossils and the earth sciences. Picking up individual fossils can be fun, exciting, and a rich learning experience, but the scientific value of a fossil depends on the context of the rocks in which it is found. The rock layers determine a fossil's age and provide clues to ancient environments. Other nearby fossils or microfossils found within **rock matrix** reveal valuable information about the entire ecology surrounding a fossil discovery. Extracting and preserving fossils from rock matrix requires experience, skill, and some training.

## FINDING FOSSILS

It is quite possible to stand on rich, fossil-bearing rock and not see a thing. Paleontologists know this. When they venture into new territory, the first thing they must do is develop a **search image** for the kinds of fossils in that area. For example, William Nothdurft, in his book *The Lost Dinosaurs of Egypt*, tells how paleontologist Peter Dodson described the process to them when they were hunting for dinosaur bone in Bahariya, Africa: "Lots of people can walk across a piece of ground and step right on fossil bone, never even see it. So when we get to a site like Bahariya, the first thing we want to do is look closely at the bone that is characteristic there. We look for the cell structure. If it looks fibrous, you know it's not a rock." Fossil bones found in that area often look dark like charred wood, sometimes with a purplish sheen. All fossil bone shows the same porous structure of live bone up close, but learning to spot the distinctive color and look of the bone from a distance makes hunting a lot easier.

People hunting for fish fossils in Green River shale look for the dark brown organic layers of mashed fish sandwiched between the light tan layers of sandstone. A blow with a rock hammer and chisel along the dark seam will often split the rock there, revealing a fish fossil. Hunting late in the day when the sun is low often shows a slight bulge in a sheet of rock that marks the location of a fossil. Many hunters start by circling around that bulge with their normal tools, then slowly use special tools to work their way through the overlying rock. Using this technique, they can uncover nearly perfect specimens.

Paleontologist Carrie Lambert uncovers 30,000-year-old fossils near a leg bone of the second largest mastodon found on North America's West Coast, at an excavation pit in California in 1997. Many mastodons have been found at the site, including the largest one found on the West Coast, named Max, discovered in 1995.

After they gain experience looking for a variety of fossils, paleontologists may decide to specialize in one area that particularly excites them. This way, they get to know one group of creatures very well and may become the local go-to person for that kind of fossil. Quite often, those fossils are the ones found close to home—perhaps those literally just beneath a collector's feet.

## Spotting Fossils at 65 Miles Per Hour

Paleontologist Kirk Johnson of the Denver Museum of Nature and Science has learned to spot dinosaur tracks while driving across U.S. western highways. He describes the process in *Cruisin' the Fossil Freeway*, an entertaining book illustrated by artist Ray Troll. "What I do is read road cuts the way you read billboards," says Johnson. Roads often cut through geological strata like a knife slices through layered birthday cake. In the Mesozoic Morrison Formation, layers of sandstone often alternate with layers of mudstone. Dinosaurs left tracks in mud that later filled with sand. In the Morrison, the mudstones tend to be deep shades of red and greenish gray while sandstones appear buckskin tan.

Imagine a sparrow running across the top of a frosted birthday cake. The sparrow would leave three-toed tracks in the frosting much like those of its theropod dinosaur ancestors. Each toe would leave a depression like a small valley in the frosting. If someone covered up the sparrow tracks with white frosting, that frosting would fill up all the toe valleys with white. Should someone cut down through those layers in the middle of a footprint, they would notice that the white frosting (just like the Morrison sandstone) dips down almost like three teeth side by side. "So tracks and trackways," Johnson says, "appear as bumps projecting off the bottom of the (sandstone) layers."

Sandstone is harder than mudstone and often "sticks out" in a road cut where the mudstone above and below has eroded away. When a sandstone slab finally breaks off, the "bumps" often wind up facedown toward the ground, meaning that anyone who flips the rock over will see a footprint cast. Of course, before the sandstone falls, Johnson knows the footprints will be found on the underside of a sandstone overhang. He impresses many amateur fossil hunters by finding new tracks and trackways with this technique, drawn from experience, knowledge of geology, and the ability to think in the third dimension.

## RECORDING AND EXTRACTING FOSSIL FINDS

Scientists must know all the details about a fossil's origin in order to successfully "read" the past. A variety of books, like *The Practical Paleontologist* by Steve Parker, describe some of the basic techniques.

Sketch maps that show the various layers, or **horizons**, at a site allow scientists to give fossils an accurate date based on comparisons with other documented sites. They look for rock features like grain size, how crumbly the layer is, the kinds of fossils in place, if any, and color of the rock. Sketch maps include measurements recording the depths of each layer. Photographs can be useful, especially if they show easily recognized landmarks. Field notebooks should also contain frame numbers and a description of the fossil captured in each photograph to easily identify them later.

Large fossil sites may be staked out using the **grid method**. Field crews place pegs at one-yard (or one-meter) intervals and connect them with string. A wooden frame that measures one-yard (or one meter) square is similarly divided into squares measuring 4 inches (or 10 cm) on a side. Someone moves this frame over each square in sequence and records on graph paper the fossils or fragments found in each smaller square. This process may have to be repeated at various depths as people remove rock from each square, so a big excavation can take a long time.

Extracting fossils can be as simple as picking them off the ground or as difficult as hauling off blocks of stone weighing tons. When blocks of limestone contain many fossils, a paleontologist can break off a chunk and treat it with dilute acids like muriatic acid (HCl) or acetic acid (vinegar). The preparer alternates acid baths with careful washing of the specimen and treatment with chemical hardeners that firm up the fossil as matrix dissolves away. Rock hammers and chisels, when used carefully by those with some experience, can reduce the size of a rock in the field. Huge fossil bones become exposed on one side and then covered by layers of burlap dipped in plaster of Paris. Field workers then undercut a hunk of stone containing the entire bone or

# Finding and Excavating Fossils 73

This 3-inch (8-cm) dinosaur tooth fragment was found exposed to air at an albertosaur site at the Dinosaur Provincial Park in Alberta, Canada.

set of bones and flip it over to repeat the process on the other side. A truck, helicopter, or other vehicle can then transport the plastered specimen to a museum or other location for further preparation.

Even during the excitement of discovery, it is important to keep careful records. Each cast, box, plastic bag, or newspaper-wrapped specimen should be clearly labeled with information that corresponds to field records. Preparation may lag behind collection for months, years, or even decades, depending on the availability of research funds, volunteers, or interest. In 2007, a fossil discovered by paleontologist Arthur Lakes in 1874 (described as a "fossil saurian tooth" and labeled YPM 4192) was finally identified as a *T. rex* tooth by Ken Carpenter at the Denver Museum of Nature and Science. The tooth had been sent to the Yale Peabody Museum (the YPM in the identification tag), but was never described in a scientific paper. It was not until 1905 that paleontologists uncovered more complete *T. rex* remains in Wyoming, and by then the saurian tooth had been forgotten. Without a well-labeled and dated specimen, however, Carpenter would never have properly linked this important specimen with its site of discovery.

## PREPARING FOR "HAPPY ACCIDENTS"

In 1922, Roy Chapman Andrews, a paleontologist with the American Museum of Natural History, led an expedition to the Gobi Desert in central Asia. Scientists of the day hoped that he might find the remains of early humans in the area. Instead, a paleontologist in the party found mammal and dinosaur bones plus eggshell fragments they thought may have belonged to some primitive bird. Rather than push on to other locations to pursue their original goal, Andrews's expedition had the good sense to realize they had found a rich, unexpected treasure. During the follow-up trip in 1923, expedition members ultimately found a total of 25 complete eggs, many of them in nests. Dinosaur bones lay close by. In one case, a dinosaur skeleton lay draped over a clutch of eggs. Andrews was the first one to find dinosaur eggs—a discovery that eventually made him famous. (Andrews is considered to be the inspiration for the fictional character Indiana Jones.) More importantly, Andrews's discovery led to many more finds and inspired new generations of fossil hunters.

Andrews's "happy accident" has been repeated many times in many ways by other paleontologists. It demonstrates an important, two-pronged lesson: Be prepared (or you may not find anything), but be open to seizing opportunity when you trip over it. It might just turn out to be even more exciting than your original goal.

Ironically, years later in 1953, a young Thomas Rich read *All About Dinosaurs*, a book written by Andrews. He became fascinated by the fact that the earliest mammalian ancestors of human beings lived literally beneath the feet of enormous dinosaurs and the story of how Andrews had found their bones. Rich marks the day he read that book as the day he decided to become a paleontologist. Years later, as a graduate student working in Australia, he decided to look for evidence of primitive mammals in that country. Instead, he found dinosaur bones. In fact, he found evidence that dinosaurs had lived in Australia when that continent still lay relatively close to Antarctica, 100 to 120 million years ago. (Although the world was warmer then, the dinosaurs [and the forests they lived in] would have experienced seasonally freezing temperatures and had to adapt to six months of darkness.)

Rich had the good sense to run with his discovery, too, and describes his decades-long work in *Dinosaurs of Darkness*. He also had the added satisfaction of discovering in some of his quarries, many years after the initial work began, the very mammal fossils he had been looking for in the first place.

## HOT SPOTS FOR FOSSILS IN THE TWENTY-FIRST CENTURY

Where have happy accidents turned up in the twenty-first century? Where are probable hot spots for new discoveries? Old sites still produce many surprises. John Foster, in his book *Jurassic West*, talks about how new dinosaurs are still turning up in exposures of the Morrison Formation in western Wyoming after more than a hundred years of exploration there. "The fact that new things can be learned and new animals found in a formation as extensively explored as the Morrison only points out how relatively little we know of what was around at the time and how the animals lived," says Foster. Likewise, Montana's Hell Creek Formation is still producing dinosaurs like the spiky-headed *Dracorex*, a kind of **pachycephalosaur**; and Dakota, a mummified hadrosaur still wrapped in a nearly complete envelope of fossilized skin.

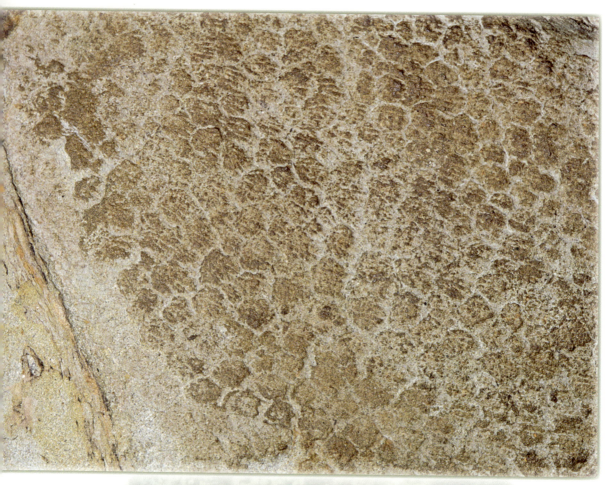

A recently discovered dinosaur mummy named Dakota has the rare distinction of including perfectly fossilized skin.

However, paleontologists continue to explore new areas as humans expand their territories and political boundaries shift. Sites in Argentina, Madagascar, North Africa, and Mongolia continue to produce new and amazing dinosaur species like *Amargasaurus* from Argentina, which has a double row of spines along its back; and *Masiakasaurus*, a German Shepherd-sized meat eater from Madagascar with an unbelievably toothy overbite. China produces an amazing array of feathered dinosaurs that continues to clarify the relationship between dinosaurs and modern birds. As we have seen, China is also producing fossils from the very dawn of complex life.

Paleontologists can also expect amazing finds to come from Venezuela. Hundreds of petroleum seeps, like the La Brea Tar Pits in Los Angeles, dot that country's landscape. The asphalt-rich goo in these pits has trapped an untold number of creatures over a period of time that stretches back two million years. The relatively small La Brea Tar Pits have produced more than a million fossils trapped during a 40,000-year time span. A sample excavation of one of the Venezuelan pits (or *menes*) in 1998 produced 43 species of mammals, 56 species of birds, 11 species of lizards, and 4 species of frogs in just one field season. In the future, these pits will document important migrations of species between North and South America and reveal how species changed as a result of the rapid climate changes associated with the ebb and flow of glaciers during our Pleistocene ice ages.

The shrinking ice of our modern world's polar regions will also expose land that has been covered in ice for millions of years. The animals and plants that flourished there, like those found by Tom Rich in Australia, might provide vital survival clues for those of us who will live to experience a much warmer twenty-first century world.

# Fossils in the Human Family

▲▲▲

HUMAN BEINGS TAKE PRIDE IN THEIR FAMILIES, EVEN IF THEY ARE NOT perfect. Call someone's mother bad names and you risk getting smacked. Thus, when Charles Darwin published his theory of evolution in 1859 in *The Origin of Species*, he did so nervously. In this book, he never discusses human evolution other than to say, "Light will be thrown on the origin of man and his history." Nevertheless, if animal species changed over time, or evolved, it was natural for people to wonder about human origins. To imply that people were once animals of some kind—most likely some kind of primate—was like calling your mother an ape to people in Darwin's time. Besides, there were few fossil primates known in the nineteenth century. But Darwin had kept lots of notes pertaining to human evolution and waited. In 1871, as support for his ideas grew, he published *The Descent of Man, and Selection in Relation to Sex* to show how natural selection applied to human evolution. Since that time, paleontologists have collected many fossils in support of his concepts, but lots of people still refuse to acknowledge apelike ancestors in the trunk of their family tree.

# Fossils in the Human Family

In this 1874 cartoon, Charles Darwin's head sits atop an ape's body—a reaction to Darwin's *The Descent of Man*, which was first published in 1871.

## MAN'S PLACE IN NATURE

In the 1690s, the English anatomist Edward Tyson dissected a chimpanzee for the first time. He was amazed at the structural similarities between chimps and humans. In 1699, he wrote that the chimp and human brain bore a "surprising" resemblance to each other and went on to say, "One would be apt to think, that since there is so great a disparity between the Soul of a Man, and a Brute, the Organ likewise in which 'tis placed should be very different, too."

Studies by primatologists like Jane Goodall have shown that chimps demonstrate love, loyalty, jealousy, and other emotions, as well as complex social relationships and intelligence once thought to be exclusively human traits. Geneticists have mapped human and chimp DNA and shown that their genetic codes differ by as little as 1%. Of course, it is important to note that humans did not evolve from chimps or any other existing ape. Each of the primates that share our world possesses its own unique family tree. Our close physical and genetic similarities do imply that we shared a common ancestor perhaps 4 to 7 million years ago—not long ago at all, at least using a geologist's wristwatch.

Darwin's arguments for human evolution in *The Descent of Man* rested largely on comparative anatomy and similarities in early development of man and other animals. Human beings bear structures like wisdom teeth and the little side passage in the gut, called an appendix, that seem to serve no apparent function and which sometimes decay or become infected, but these **vestigial organs** do reflect past history. These leftover structures functioned in some way for our animal ancestors and were passed along the chain of inheritance. Human embryos develop with tails and gills that echo those used by distant fishy forebears that swam in Paleozoic seas. Today, those who specialize in studying human evolution can also examine hundreds if not thousands of actual fossils our ancestors and close relatives left behind during the last several million years.

Scientists now place all apes and humans in the same "superfamily" called the Hominoidea. Humans (and their extinct relatives), chimps, and gorillas share enough similarities to be placed in the common family Hominidae. Humans, both modern and extinct, have their own "tribe" within the Hominidae family called the Hominini. Thus, various members of this scientific tribe are called **hominins**. The collection of hominin fossils grows larger each year. They demonstrate that human evolution resembles a berry bush that has been trimmed over time to the one branch on which we all dangle.

## MISSING LINKS, MISSING BRANCHES

Perhaps the most famous hominin remains were discovered in a German cave in the Neander Valley in 1857, two years before *The Origin of Species* was published. The bones certainly looked quite human, with a brutish sort of flare. The thick limb bones spoke of hard use by those who possessed them. A ridge of bone shielded the eye sockets like the brim of a cap. One early description depicted the living man who belonged to these bones as a stooped and half-human "ape man," an image that stuck for a hundred years. Today, we know that the first bones described belonged to a fairly old individual suffering from arthritis. Others must have fed and cared for him. These **Neandertals**, now given the scientific name *Homo neanderthalensis*, made and used complex tools, butchered and cooked food, and buried their dead with evidence of respect and ceremony. They lived in Europe (and perhaps as far east as Siberia) between 130,000 and 27,000 years ago, coexisting on the Arabian Peninsula and southern Europe with fully modern humans toward the end of their existence as a species.

In 1997, it became possible to extract small samples of DNA from Neandertal bones. Sequencing that DNA and comparing it to modern humans indicates that our common ancestor lived more than a half-million years ago. Neandertals developed from an **archaic** version of human beings forced to adapt to climatic "spasms" in Europe that involved the advance and retreat of huge glaciers over a period of several hundred thousand years. But our common ancestor lived farther south. Fossil and DNA evidence both imply that the continent of Africa served as home to many of the species that would contribute to the human story.

Our species name, *Homo sapiens*, literally means "man, the wise." We admire ourselves for being new and quite unique, but we really are an evolutionary patchwork. "The human we see in today's mirror," says Christopher Sloan, author of *Smithsonian*

## Watch Where You Step

In 1976, on an African field trip at a site called Laetoli, two young scientists got bored and starting throwing elephant dung chips at each other. (In his book *Lucy: The Beginnings of Humankind*, paleontologist Donald Johanson explained that sometimes there is not much to do on remote digs.) One fellow, Andrew Hill, while ducking an elephant dung pie and looking for another, discovered what appeared to be animal tracks in a volcanic ash layer in the dry streambed on which he was standing. The pie fight stopped and the tracks were confirmed, but the site could not be excavated until the following year.

In 1977, Mary Leakey and members of her scientific team discovered elephant and other animal tracks at the same site. Among those tracks were a pair that looked like they might have been made by a hominin, but it would take some effort to completely expose the delicate layer of ash in which they were impressed. At first Leakey gave fossil bone hunting priority over the track excavation, but as paleontologist Tim White exposed more and more tracks, excitement grew among the rest of the crew. Ultimately, over several field seasons, 70 recognizable footprints emerged in a path nearly 80 feet (24 meters) long. "Make no mistake about it," said White. "They are like modern human footprints. If one were left in the sand of a California beach today, and a four-year-old were asked what it was, he would instantly say that somebody had walked there."

## Fossils in the Human Family

*Intimate Guide to Human Origins*, "is like a mosaic of many tiles, some extremely old and some very new." One of our oldest features, it turns out, is the way we walk. A 3.2-million-year-old fossil skeleton nicknamed "Lucy" (after lyrics in a popular Beatles song) and a set of incredible trace fossils confirms this idea. Lucy's limb and hip bones implied that she walked upright. Parallel tracks

Here is what happened: 3.7 million years ago, Sadiman, a now-extinct volcano, belched a puff of volcanic ash that deposited about a half-inch of fine cinders. Then it rained and the ash turned into natural, gooey cement. The sky cleared, the ash dried a little, and then a bunch of animals—including elephants, giraffes, rhinos, pigs, birds—walked on it . . . including at least two hominins who walked close together, perhaps nervously eyeing the volcano that had scared them a short time before. Then, the tracks dried, and the volcano belched again, preserving them with another ash layer until a game of "throw the elephant dung" many years later.

An interpreter points out the 3.7-million-year-old hominin footprints that were fossilized in volcanic rock to a group of Masai women at the Laetoli site in northern Tanzania.

that are 3.7 million years old proved that two individuals about Lucy's size left hauntingly human footprints behind them.

Lucy was given the scientific name *Australopithecus afarensis*, which means "southern ape of the Afar region." Lucy probably looked more like an ape than a human except for the way she walked. Several other species of *Australopithecus* lived in Africa over a period of 1.5 million years. There is no evidence that any of these species ventured beyond Africa. A species of hominin named *Homo habilis* lived in roughly the same territory as Lucy about 2 million years ago. They made simple stone tools and had somewhat larger brains. They, too, stayed in Africa. A species named *Homo erectus* made the first early and extensive migrations out of Africa, equipped with a sturdy body, bigger brain, and, eventually, the ability to use fire.

## OUT OF AFRICA

In 1984, Kamoya Kimeu and Richard Leakey (the son of Mary Leakey) found the nearly complete skeleton of a young *Homo erectus* boy in Kenya. His body looked completely human in proportion, but had somewhat thicker bones. This "Nariokotome boy" (sometimes called "Turkana boy") lived 1.6 million years ago. He stood about 5 feet 3 inches (1.6 meters) tall—probably close to his full growth height—and had suffered from a bad tooth infection. He may have been as young as seven years old. This kind of rapid early growth is more typical of apes. While his body looked very "modern," his skull, like that of all *H. erectus*, did not. He had a brain about the size of a one-year-old child living today, housed in a skull with heavy brow ridges and a projecting face. Based on some skull features, it is thought that *H. erectus* probably could not talk as we do.

Although Nariokotome Boy lived in Africa, the remains of his species have been found from Java and Indonesia to China and Eurasia. His kind used their long legs and skills with toolmaking to leave Africa and sample what the rest of the world had to offer during an extended period of mild climate. Their skills served them well. They existed from at least 2 million years ago to half a million years ago. Newly discovered fossils of a pygmy race that

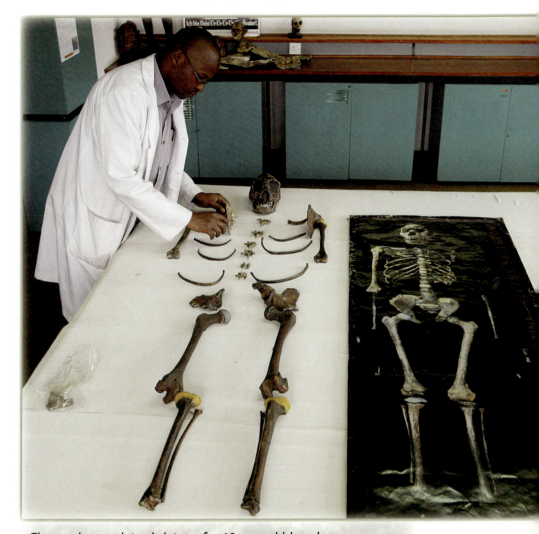

The nearly complete skeleton of a 12-year-old boy, known as Nariokotome Boy, is displayed by research scientist Samuel Muteti at Kenya National Museum in Nairobi. The skeleton is 1.6 million years old.

lived on the island of Flores, near Indonesia, as late as 18,000 years ago may represent the last of their variety of human.

But, in the old African homeland, most likely coming from *H. erectus* stock, a new species equipped with a significantly larger brain evolved about 700,000 years ago. These **archaic**

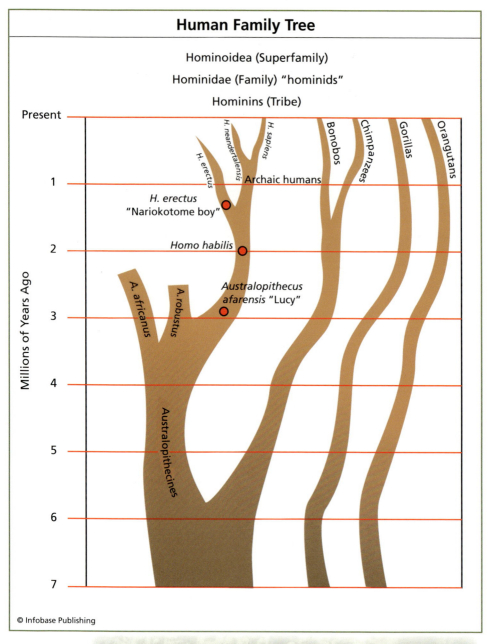

This example of a probable human family tree shows how our closest primate relatives split off in branches at different points in evolutionary history.

**humans** also ventured out of Africa during a warm spell, with one branch developing into the Neandertals of Europe. It is hard to imagine the comings and goings of species that existed so long ago and for stretches of time that dwarf all of modern history, but these humans, like people today, moved to wherever they could best survive and prosper. During times of cool climates, when lots of seawater lay frozen in glaciers to the north, sea levels fell and new territory opened up. In warm, wet times, forests expanded. People followed the dictates of their stomachs and slowly hunted, fished, and otherwise ate their way around the world.

How did these various hominins interact? Could they and did they interbreed? Did they fight or avoid each other? Scientists now debate such details, and others, as new fossil evidence comes to light and genetic studies of modern human populations continue.

It is important to remember that scientists debate the details of human evolution, not the fact that it occurred. Evolution by natural selection serves as the cornerstone of biology the way Newton's laws of motion anchor our understanding of physics.

## OUT OF AFRICA—AGAIN

Paleontologists and **anthropologists** (scientists who specialize in the study of human remains, both physical and cultural) pretty much had the study of human prehistory to themselves until chemists realized that the DNA tucked into each and every one of our cells represents a fantastic library of past events—specifically mistakes (mutations) in copying DNA from generation to generation. While such goof-ups are usually bad news, mutations provide gene variations that sometimes have survival value. They create evolutionary change. Not only that, the mutations hang around to serve as markers that can show when some populations split from others.

In January 2008, for example, European scientists discovered that a specific mutation in the gene that codes for the dark pigment melanin occurred only about 8,000 years ago. The mutation reduced the amount of melanin in the iris of the eye, producing the first blue-eyed individuals. Scientists made their claim based on studying certain DNA that is easy to track: **mitochondrial DNA**. Mitochondrial DNA, which is located in the energy-producing organelles (mitochondria) of women's egg cells, can be tracked from mothers to daughters. The amount of time that has passed since a mutation occurred can be estimated based on changes in the DNA near the mutation site. The more variation in DNA around the mutation site, the more time has passed.

DNA on the Y chromosome of men passes only from father to son. This DNA, too, can be tracked fairly easily. The dumpy little Y chromosome partners with an X chromosome to make a guy a guy. (Women have two X chromosomes.) The Y does not carry a lot of genetic information, but errors in the genes it does carry are uniquely male.

Geneticists like Bryan Sykes at Oxford University have been tracking female ancestry following mutations in mitochondrial DNA. Geneticist Spencer Wells and others have been tracking Y chromosome DNA. Studies from both groups have come up with similar results. The most genetic variety and the oldest mutations come from African populations—implying that we are all Africans. Other mutations occurred as humans spread across the planet. By sampling isolated populations from all over the world, they have been able to create maps of human migration and evolution. Secondly, their studies indicate that every single modern population of human beings alive today descended from a population that lived in Africa about 200,000 years ago—in other words, they are our grandparents 10,000 times removed.

About 125,000 years ago, a period of favorable climate allowed humans to migrate out of Africa again. Archaic Africans occupied territory in what is now modern Israel and Lebanon and may have encountered Neandertals. In fact, caves in this region contain the remains of both species, usually in distinct layers, yet some skeletons show hints of mixed character traits. Then the climate deteriorated again, either forcing these people back to Africa or destroying them. Humans again left Africa 85,000 to 90,000 years ago when the climate was right. They spread throughout the world as *H. erectus* had done so long before. Nature provided one more surprise for early humans 71,000 years ago. The volcano of Toba on the island of Sumatra erupted with a violence 700 times greater than Mount St. Helens in 1980. Data from ice cores and measurements of ash layers in India and elsewhere indicate that 6 years of global winter were followed by a thousand years of harsh climate. Worldwide, human populations may have crashed to just a few thousand individuals. But perhaps—although there is no way to know for sure—this, and other similar crises, may have helped forge another change in the people who survived to become us.

## THE IMAGINATION RENAISSANCE

Humans may have walked for 6 million years, made tools for more than 2 million years, and possessed essentially the same body and brain size for nearly 200,000 years, but many scientists see something unique in human behavior that appeared between 70,000 and 50,000 years ago. These examples of modern behaviors include

- the making of finely crafted projectile points and other tools that are not only made with care and attention to detail, but vary from region to region;
- long-distance trading for raw materials;
- the making of harpoons, sewing needles, awls, and other tools with very specific purposes from bone, bamboo, and other materials;
- the creation of art in the form of jewelry and, later, in the form of cave paintings and rock art.

These behaviors imply the abilities of abstract thinking, planning for future events, innovation, and the use of symbols to represent concepts that together create human culture. In short, humans became capable of imagination—a trait that even Einstein recognized was more important than knowledge. We cannot plan for and shape a future that we cannot first imagine.

### WHAT'S NEXT FOR US, THE "FUTURE FOSSILS"?

We human beings have reached the point in our understanding of our environment that we are capable of shaping at least some of our own evolution. Whether we will, or even whether we should, tinker with such powers are questions that we, as a species, should ask ourselves, using all the tools of reason, philosophy, and spiritual insight that we can bring to bear.

The fossils tell us that life somehow arose from humble chemical interactions to evolve into a highly complex network of living things all intertwined and interdependent. Genes combine, recombine, duplicate, and mutate, to manifest themselves, temporarily, as creatures, some of which leave traces behind that we, the "imagining ones," read with imperfection. But as imperfect as the fossil story is, paleontologists pore over its pages with a sense of wonder and amazement born of a 4-billion-year journey that is far from completed.

# Glossary

**Absolute time scale**   Time scale that is measurable in years.
**Agate**   Rock of mixed colors composed of silicon dioxide ($SiO_2$).
**Amber**   Fossilized tree sap (resin).
**Ammonite**   An extinct mollusk with a coiled shell.
**Angiosperms**   Flowering plants.
**Angular unconformity**   Two layers of rock at sharp angles to one another.
**Anthropologists**   Scientists who study human physical and cultural remains.
**Aragonite**   A form of calcium carbonate ($CaCO_3$) used in shell construction.
**Archaea**   Simple organisms that lived during the Archean Eon.
**Archaeologists**   Scientists who study human tools and other artifacts.
**Archaic**   Extremely old.
**Archaic humans**   Group of humans that lived in Africa about 700,000 year ago.
**Archean eon**   Period of time from 4 to 2.5 billion years ago.
**Atomic clocks**   Radioactive elements whose decay rate can be used to determine a fossil's age.
**Banded iron formation**   Group of Precambrian rocks with high iron content.
**Burgess Shale**   Important early Cambrian fossil site in British Columbia, Canada.

**Calcite** A form of the mineral calcium carbonate.
**Cambrian Explosion** Rapid diversification of life that began 540 million years ago.
**Carbonization** Preservation of an organism as a thin carbon film.
**Casts** Preservation of the overall shape and exterior detail of an organism.
**Catastrophism** Theory that fossils change drastically at times because of major catastrophes that destroy most living things.
**Cenozoic Era** Period of time from 65 million years ago to the present.
**Chordate** An animal that possess a nerve chord along its back.
**Conifers** Seed plants with cones, like pine trees.
**Contour lines** Lines on a geological map that indicate elevation.
**Coprolite** Fossilized dung.
**Cycads** Primitive seed plants that flourished in the Mesozoic Era.
**Darwin, Charles** Nineteenth-century scientist who convincingly described the process of evolution through mutation and natural selection.
**Deposition** Gradual accumulation of sediments at the bottom of a water column.
**DNA (Deoxyribonucleic acid)** The compound that serves as the genetic code for organisms.
**Ediacarans** Sheet- or leaflike marine creatures that lived just prior to the Cambrian Period.
**Eons** The largest blocks of geological time, measured in billions of years.
**Epochs** Subdivisions of time within eras.
**Eras** Subdivisions of time within eons.
**Erosion** Process of breaking up and carrying away rocks by the actions of wind, water, and temperature changes.

# Glossary

**Evolution** Transformation of species over time through mutation and natural selection.
**Extinction** Permanent loss of a species of organism.
**Formations** Groups of rocks of similar appearance and origin.
**Fossils** The physical remains or traces of once-living things, usually mineralized.
**Geological maps** Maps designed to show the geological features of an area.
**Geological time** Time spans long enough to measure mountain building and other geological processes.
**Geology** The scientific study of rocks, minerals, and geological forces.
**Green River Formation** Fossil-rich rocks of a region in the American West formed by an ancient system of freshwater lakes.
**Grid method** Dividing a fossil dig site into squares in order to map discoveries.
**Hadrosaurs** Vegetarian "duck-billed" dinosaurs of the Cretaceous Period.
**Hominins** Fossil primates believed to be the ancestors of modern humans.
**Horizons** Distinctive layers of rock within a formation.
**Igneous rocks** Rocks formed under extreme heat and pressure.
**Index fossils** Fossils useful in marking relatively short intervals of geological time.
**Iridium** Rare element used as a marker for impacts of large meteors and asteroids (in which iridium is abundant).
**KT boundary** Boundary between the Cretaceous and Tertiary periods.
**Living fossils** Animals currently alive that closely resemble fossil species.
**Lycopods** Primitive plants that grew to tree size during the Paleozoic Era.

**Macroscopic**  An object that is visible without magnification.
**Mass extinction events**  Periods of time during which a large number of species disappear from the fossil record within a relatively short time.
**Mesozoic Era**  Period of time from 251 to 65 million years ago (The Age of Dinosaurs).
**Meteorites**  Extraterrestrial objects that strike the Earth; large ones are called asteroids.
**Microfossils**  Microscopic fossils.
**Microscopic**  An object that is visible only with magnification.
**Mitochondrial DNA**  DNA found in the mitochondria of cells.
**Mold**  Impression of a living thing in rock. (Casts are made using molds.)
**Molten**  Melted rock.
**Morrison Formation**  Jurassic Age group of reddish rocks common in the American West.
**Mudstone**  Mud turned to stone under heat and pressure.
**Mummy**  Dried or freeze-dried remains of a once-living thing.
**Natural selection**  Selection by nature of only the most fit organisms to reproduce.
**Neandertals**  Archaic, now-extinct humans who lived in Europe and Asia during several periods of glaciation.
**Pachycephalosaurs**  Type of Cretaceous dinosaurs with bony head shields.
**Paleobotanist**  Paleontologist who studies fossil plants.
**Paleontologist**  Scientist who studies fossils.
**Paleozoic Era**  Period of time from 542 to 251 million years ago.
**Periods**  Subdivisions of geological eras.
**Permineralization**  Crystallization of minerals out of solution as water evaporates.
**Petrified**  Commonly used term to describe the mineralization of wood.

# Glossary

**Phanerozoic Eon**  The period of time from 542 million years ago to the present.

**Precambrian**  Geological time from the origin of the Earth until 542 million years ago.

**Principle of original horizontality**  Sediments were level when first deposited.

**Principle of superposition**  Older sediments lie beneath younger ones.

**Proterozoic Eon**  Period of time from 2.5 billion years ago to 542 million years ago.

**Pseudomorph**  A fossil cast having only the shape and outer impression of a tree or other organism.

**Pterosaurs**  Extinct flying reptiles of the Mesozoic Era.

**Quartz**  White, often translucent mineral made of silicon dioxide.

**Radioactivity**  Emission of X-rays by an element.

**Relative time**  Age of a fossil or formation as compared to another fossil or formation.

**Replacement**  When inorganic minerals replace organic compounds during fossilization.

**Resin**  Tree sap.

**Rock matrix**  The rock surrounding a fossil.

**Sandstone**  Stone formed from compressed and heated sand.

**Sauropod**  Long-necked vegetarian dinosaur.

**Scanning electron microscope**  Microscope using electrons rather than light to form an image of small objects.

**Search image**  Mental image of what to look for in the field.

**Sedimentary rock**  Rock formed from the heating and compression of sediments originally laid down in water.

**Shale**  Sedimentary rock with a high clay content.

**Shocked quartz**  Quartz modified by the extreme heat and pressure of a large meteorite or asteroid.

**Silt**  A deposit of mud or fine soil at the bottom of standing water.

**Steno, Nicolaus**  Seventeenth century scientist who recognized fossils as the remains of once-living creatures and who outlined basic geological processes.

**Strata**  Rock layers.

**Stromatolites**  Fossilized colonies of primitive organisms called cyanobacteria.

**Subsided**  Sunken.

**Tar pits**  Holes filled with thickened natural asphalt produced by organic sediments.

**Terrestrial**  Pertaining to dry land.

**Tetrapods**  Four-legged animals.

**Theropods**  Predatory dinosaurs that walked on two legs, like *T. rex*.

**Topography**  The shape of the land, including mountains, valleys, and plains.

**Trace fossil**  Anything a living creature leaves behind as fossils, such as tracks and droppings.

**Uniformitarianism**  Theory that geological forces acted in the past much as they do today.

**United States Geological Survey (USGS)**  Government agency that maps and surveys geological features in the United States.

**Uplift**  Rising of large landmasses.

**Uranium**  Radioactive element used for geological time measurements.

**Vestigial organs**  Organs that no longer perform their original function.

**Volcanic ash**  Soot produced by erupting volcanoes.

**X-rays**  Radiation produced when the atoms of an element emits subatomic particles.

# Bibliography

Albritton, Claude C. *The Abyss of Time*. Los Angeles: Jeremy P. Tarcher, Inc., 1986.

Alvarez, Walter. *T. rex and the Crater of Doom*. Princeton, New Jersey: Princeton University Press, 1995.

Bower, B. "Going Coastal: Sea Cave Yields Ancient Signs of Modern Behavior." *Science News*, Vol. 172, No. 16, (Oct. 20, 2007): pp. 243–244.

Briggs, Derek, E. G., Douglas H. Erwin, and Frederick J. Collier. *The Fossils of the Burgess Shale*. Washington and London: Smithsonian Institution Press, 1994.

Bryner, Jeanna. "Genetic Mutation Makes Those Brown Eyes Blue." Live Science. Available online. Accessed February 15, 2008. URL: http://www.msnbc.msn.com/id/22934464/wid/11915773?GT1=10815.

Burchfield, Joe D. *Lord Kelvin and the Age of the Earth*. Chicago and London: The University of Chicago Press, 1990.

Cadbury, Deborah. *Terrible Lizard*. New York: Henry Holt and Company, 2000.

Chin, Karen, Timothy T. Tokaryk, Gregory M. Erickson, and Lewis C. Calk. "A King-sized Theropod Coprolite Found in Saskatchewan." *Nature* 393 (June 18, 1998): pp. 680–682.

Clos, Lynne M. *Field Adventures in Paleontology*. Boulder, Colo.: Fossil News, 2003.

Cutler, Alan. *The Seashell on the Mountaintop*. New York: Dutton, 2003.

Fortey, Richard. *Earth, An Intimate History*. New York: Alfred A. Knopf, 2004.

Foster, John. *Jurassic West, The Dinosaurs of the Morrison Formation and Their World*. Bloomington and Indianapolis: Indiana University Press, 2007.

Garrett, Kenneth. *The Human Story*. Washington, D.C.: *National Geographic*, (2004): pp. 36–49.

Gore, Rick. "Dinosaurs." *National Geographic* 183, No. 1 (1993): pp. 2–53.

Gould, Stephen Jay. *Time's Arrow, Time's Cycle*. Cambridge, Mass.: Harvard University Press, 1987.

Gould, Stephen Jay. *Wonderful Life*. New York: W.W. Norton & Company, 1989.

Grande, Lance. *Paleontology of the Green River Formation, With a Review of the Fish Fauna*. Bulletin 63, Geological Survey of Wyoming, 1980.

Hall, Stephen S. "Last Hours of the Iceman." *National Geographic* 212, No. 3 (2007): pp. 68–81.

Jefferson, Thomas. *The Writings of Thomas Jefferson*. Andrew A. Lipscomb, Editor-in-Chief. Washington, D.C.: The Thomas Jefferson Memorial Association, 1904.

Johanson, Donald and Maitland Edey. *Lucy: The Beginnings of Humankind*. New York: Simon and Schuster, 1981.

Johanson, Donald and James Shrieve. *Lucy's Child: The Discovery of a Human Ancestor*. New York: William Morrow and Co., Inc., 1989.

Johnson, Kirk and Ray Troll. *Cruisin' the Fossil Freeway*. Golden, Colo.: Fulcrum Publishing, 2007.

Johnson, Kirk R. and Robert G. Raynolds. *Ancient Denvers*. Denver: Denver Museum of Nature and Science, 2002.

King, Russell, Ed. *Atlas of Human Migration*. New York: Firefly Books, Ltd., 2007.

Lewis, Cherry. *The Dating Game*. Cambridge, UK: Cambridge University Press, 2000.

Lockley, Martin. *A Guide to the Fossil Footprints of the World*. Morrison, Colo.: A Lockley-Peterson Publication, 2002.

Mayor, Adrienne. *The First Fossil Hunters: Paleontology in Greek and Roman Times*. Princeton, New Jersey: Princeton University Press, 2001.

McMenamin, Mark A.S. *The Garden of Ediacara*. New York: Columbia University Press, 1998.

McPhee, John. *Basin and Range*. New York: Farrar, Straus, and Giroux, 1981.

Meyer, Herbert W. *The Fossils of Florissant*. Washington and London: Smithsonian Books, 2003.

Natural History Museum of Los Angeles County. "Reconstructing a Late Pleistocene Environment." *Terra* 31, No. 1, (Fall 1992): pp. 12–27.

Nothdurft, William. *The Lost Dinosaurs of Egypt*. New York: Random House, 2002.

Osborn, Henry Fairfield. "Thomas Jefferson as a Paleontologist." *Science*, Vol. 82, No. 2136, (Dec. 6, 1935): pp. 533–538.

Parker, Steve and Raymond Bernor, eds. *The Practical Paleontologist*. New York: Simon and Schuster, Inc., 1990.

Perkins, Sid. "La Brea Del Sur." *Science News*, Vol. 173, No. 2 (January 12, 2008): pp. 24–26.

Poinar, George Jr. and Roberta Poinar. *The Amber Forest*. Princeton, N.J: Princeton University Press, 1999.

Raham, R. Gary. *Explorations in Backyard Biology*. Portsmouth, N.H.: Teacher Ideas Press, 1996.

Rich, Thomas H. and Patricia Vickers-Rich. *Dinosaurs of Darkness*. Bloomington and Indianapolis, Ind.: Indiana University Press, 2000.

Rogers, Katherine. *The Sternberg Fossil Hunters: A Dinosaur Dynasty*. Missoula, Mont.: Mountain Press Publishing Company, 1991.

Rutherford, Ernest (Lord Rutherford Nelson), "Radium—the cause of earth's heat"; *Harper's Magazine*, 1905: February, pp. 390–396.

Sawyer, G.J., and Viktor Deak. *The Last Human*. New Haven and London: Yale University Press, 2007.

Seldon, Paul and John Nudds. *Evolution of Fossil Ecosystems*. Chicago: The University of Chicago Press, 2004.

Simpson, George Gaylord. *Fossils and the History of Life*. New York: Scientific American Books, 1983.

Spindler, Konrad. *The Man in the Ice*. New York: Harmony Books, 1994.

Sykes, Bryan. *The Seven Daughters of Eve*. New York: W.W. Norton and Co., 2001.

Thompson, Keith S. *Living Fossil: The Story of the Coelacanth*. New York: W.W. Norton and Company, 1991.

Turney, Chris. *Bones, Rocks, & Stars*. New York: Macmillan, 2006.

The United States Geological Service (USGS). "Index Fossils." Available online. URL: http://pubs.usgs.gov/gip/geotime/fossils.html. Accessed December 5, 2007.

Updike, John. "Extreme Dinosaurs." *National Geographic* 212, No. 6, (2007): pp. 32–57.

Ward, Peter D., Ph.D. *Under a Green Sky*. New York: HarperCollins Publishers, 2007.

Wells, Dr. Spencer. *Journey of Man*. Tigress Productions (PBS Home Video), 2003.

Wilson, Edward O., Ed. *From So Simple a Beginning: The Four Great Books of Charles Darwin*. New York: W.W. Norton and Co., 2006.

Winchester, Simon. *The Map That Changed the World*. New York: HarperCollins Publishers, 2001.

Womack, Todd. "Plentifully Charged With Fossils: The 1822 Discovery." in *Fossil News*, Vol. 6, No. 7 (July 2000). pp. 14–16.

Zimmer, Carl. *Smithsonian Intimate Guide to Human Origins*. Toronto, Ontario, Canada: Madison Press Books (Smithsonian Books), 2005.

# Further Reading

## BOOKS

Bergen, David. *Life-Size Dinosaurs*. New York: Sterling Publishing Company, Inc., 2004.

Bonner, Hannah. *When Bugs Were Big, Plants Were Strange, and Tetrapods Stalked the Earth*. Washington, D.C.: National Geographic, 2003.

Diamond, Judy, ed. *Virus and the Whale, Exploring Evolution in Creatures Large and Small*. Arlington, Va: NSTA Press, 2006.

Fraden, Dennis. Illustrated by Tom Newsom. *Mary Anning, The Fossil Hunter*. Parsippany, N.J.: Silver Press, 1998.

Gillette, J. Lynett. *Dinosaur Ghosts, The Mystery of Coelophysis*. New York: Dial Books for Young Readers, 1997.

Halls, Kelly Milner. *Dinosaur Mummies*. Plain City, Ohio: Darby Creek Publishing, 2003.

Henderson, Douglas. *Asteroid Impact*. New York: Dial Books for Young Readers, 2000.

Kerley, Barbara. Illustrated by Brian Selznick. *The Dinosaurs of Waterhouse Hawkins*. New York: Scholastic Press, 2001.

Manning, Dr. Phillip Lars. *Dinomummy: The Life, Death, and Discovery of Dakota, A Dinosaur from Hell Creek*. Boston: Kingfisher, 2007.

McNamara, Ken. *We Came from Slime*. New York: Annick Press, 2006.

Raham, Gary. *The Deep Time Diaries*. Golden, Colo.: Fulcrum Publishing, 2000.

———. "Dinosaur Eggcitement." *Read*, Issue 9 (January 7, 2000).

———. "The Dinosaur Mummy." *Highlights for Children.* (February 2000): pp. 30–31.

———. "Magic Tooth and the Dinosaurs." *Highlights for Children.* (November 1996): pp. 38–39.

## WEB SITES

**Denver Museum of Nature and Science: "Follow a Fossil."**
http://www.dmns.org/main/minisites/fossil/indcx.html
*Discover how paleontologists find fossils, unearth them, and prepare them for display.*

**"Ancient Denvers"**
http://www.dmns.org/main/minisites/ancientdenvers/index.html
*Views of Denver at different times in the geologic past.*

**Friends of Dinosaur Ridge**
http://www.dinoridge.org
*Learn about one of the most famous dinosaur fossil excavation sites, and read about many dinosaur-related activities and events.*

**Museum of the Earth**
http://www.museumoftheearth.org
*Provides access to the Paleontological Research Institution (PRI).*

**San Diego Natural History Museum: "Fossil Mysteries"**
http://www.sdnhm.org/exhibits/mystery/fg_giantsloth.html
*Field guide to Harlan's ground sloth. Description, ecology, and references to other information on this Ice Age ground sloth.*

**University of California Museum of Paleontology: "Fossils: Window to the Past"**
http://ucmp.berkeley.edu/paleo/fossils/
*Learn about the different kinds of fossils, how age is determined, and how fossils form.*

**University of California Museum of Paleontology: "Getting Into the Fossil Record."**
http://ucmp.berkeley.edu/education/explorations/tours/fossils/
An educational module.

**"Tour of Geologic Time."**
http://www.ucmp.berkeley.edu/exhibits/geologictime.php
*Learn about any period of geologic time by clicking on a timeline; discover information about the history of the geologic time scale and view an exhibit on plate tectonics.*

**U.S. Geological Survey**
http://www.usgs.gov
*Geological maps.*

**Western Interior Paleontological Society**
http://www.wipsppc.com
*This organization of amateur paleontologists includes membership benefits such as field trips, symposia, and other events. There are links to other sites and related information.*

# Picture Credits

▲

**Page**
10: Vanni/Art Resource, NY
11: © Kevin Schafer/CORBIS
13: © The Granger Collection, New York
16: © Jonathan Blair/CORBIS
24: AP Images
26: Howard Grey/Getty Images
28: © Tom Bean/CORBIS
29: Jeff Foott/Getty Images
31: © DK Limited/CORBIS
33: © Infobase Publishing
35: © Jim Wark/Visuals Unlimited
39: © Dr. Marli Miller/Visuals Unlimited
44: E. R. Degginger/Photo Researchers, Inc.
48: © Infobase Publishing
51: © Infobase Publishing
53: Dave Watts/Minden Pictures
57: © Infobase Publishing
62: Ken Lucas/Visuals Unlimited, Inc.
68: Spring Mount Communications
70: David McNew/Getty Images
73: Louie Psihoyos/Getty Images
76: Ken Lucas/Getty Images
79: HIP/Art Resource, NY
83: SUSAN LINNEE/AP Images
85: SAYYID AZIM/AP Images
86: © Infobase Publishing

# Index

## A
absolute time scale, 44
Africa, 82–84, 85, 87, 88–89
agate, 32
*All About Dinosaurs* (Andrews), 75
*Allosaurus,* 34, 59
Alps, 23
Alvarez, Lewis, 63
Alvarez, Walter, 63, 64
*Amargasaurus,* 76
amber, 19, 25
*The Amber Forest* (Poinar and Poinar), 25
American Federation of Mineralogical Societies (AFMS), 67
ammonites, 15, 42–43
anatomists, 12, 80
anatomy, 16, 80
Andrews, Roy Chapman, 11, 74
angular unconformities, 38, 39–40
Anning, Joseph, 15
Anning, Mary, 15
*Anomalocaris,* 56–57, 58
*Apatosaurus,* 59, 60
aragonite, 32
Araripe Basin, 58
Archaea, 54
Archean Eon, 47
atomic clocks, 47
*Australopithecus afarensis,* 84

## B
bacteria
    as decomposer, 23, 30
    preservation and, 27
Bactrians, 10
baculites, 42–43
Baltic Sea shores, 61
banded iron formations, 54
*Basin and Range* (McPhee), 38
Briggs, Derek, 56
Buckland, William, 15–16
Burchfield, Joe D., 46
Burgess Shale (Canadian Rockies), 56–58
burial speed, 27

## C
Cadbury, Deborah, 15
*Camarosaurus,* 59
Cambrian Explosion, 57
Canadian Rockies, 55–58
carbonization, 27–28
Carpenter, Ken, 74
casts, 32, 34
catastrophism theory, 17
Cenozoic Era, 47, 52, 61–63
chimpanzees, 80, 81
China, 76–77
chordates, 57
Christian beliefs
    about fossils, 9
    catastrophism theory, 17
    nature as unchanging, 14
Clark, William, 18
climate change, 64–65
clubs, 67–69
coccoliths, 43
coelacanth, 17
conodonts, 43
Cope, Edward Drinker, 60, 62
coprolites, 36
Cretaceous Period, 52, 63

*Cruisin' the Fossil Freeway* (Johnson and Troll), 71
Curie, Marie, 45
Curie, Pierre, 45
Cutler, Alan, 9
Cuvier, Georges, 16–17
Cyclopes, 8

## D

D-Worlds, described, 23
Dakota (mummified hadrosaur), 75
Darmstadt, Germany, 61
Darwin, Charles
    evolution of man and, 78, 80
    Lyell and, 41
    natural selection and, 17
deep time, numbers in, 38
deposition, 23, 40
*The Descent of Man and Selection in Relation to Sex* (Darwin), 78, 80
dinosaur fossils
    in Australia, 75
    coprolites, 36
    dinosaur defined, 19
    early discoveries, 19
    eggs, 74
    feathered in China, 76–77
    griffins and, 10
    in Mongolia, 10–11
    in Morrison Formation, 34, 58–59, 60, 71, 75
    mummified, 30–31
    recent discoveries, 19, 76
    war between Marsh and Cope, 60
Dinosaur National Monument, Utah, 59
dinosaur tracks, 34, 36, 71
*Dinosaurs of Darkness* (Rich), 75
*Diplodocus*, 59
dissections
    by Cuvier, 16
    by Steno, 9, 12
    by Tyson, 80
DNA (deoxyribonucleic acid)
    African connection, 81–84
    of chimpanzees, 80
    mutations, 87–88
    Neandertal, 81
    preserved by amber, 25
Dodson, Peter, 69
Douglass, Earl, 59, 60
*Dracorex*, 75
dung, fossilized, 36

## E

E-Worlds, described, 22–23
Earth
    age of, 44–47
    fossils provide information about history of, 20
    recycling on, 22
Ediacarans, 54
eggs, fossilized, 36–37, 74
eons, described, 47
erosion
    angular unconformities and, 40
    exposure of fossils by, 23
    Uniformitarianism and, 41
Evans, John, 61–62
evolution
    in Cenozoic Era, 61
    fossils provide information about, 20–21
    of humans, 78, 81–85, 87
    during Mesozoic Era, 58
    during Paleozoic Era, 55
    during Precambrian, 53
    during Proterozoic Era, 54
extinctions
    catastrophism theory and, 17
    climate change and, 64–65
    fossils provide information about, 20
    mass, 52, 63–64

## F

"false forms," 32
Ferdinando II (Grand Duke of Florence), 9, 12
Fickle, Charles, 7, 8
*The First Fossil Hunters* (Mayor), 10
Flinders Ranges, Australia, 54
Flores, 19–20, 84–85
Florissant, Colorado, 27–28
footprints
    casts of, 34
    dinosaur, 34, 36, 71
    hominin, 82, 83–84
foraminifera, 43
fossil hunters
    age of rocks and discoveries, 16–17

clubs for, 67–69
early, 15, 17, 19, 61–62
geological maps and, 67
*See also specific individuals*
fossilization, described, 23
fossils
described, 7
index, 42–43
information learned from, 20–21
origin of word, 8
recording and extracting, 72–74
trace, 33–34
Foster, John, 75
Friends of Dinosaur Ridge, 34

## G
Galileo, 9
geological maps, 67
Ghost Ranch, New Mexico, 58
giant ground sloth skeletons, 25
Gobi Desert, Asia, 74
Goodall, Jane, 80
Gould, Stephen Jay, 40, 57
graptolites, 43
Greeks, ancient, 8–9, 10
Green River (U.S.) fish fossils, 62, 69
grid method, 72
griffins, 10

## H
hadrosaurs, 60
*Hallucigenia*, 57–58
*Harper's Magazine*, 45–46
Hell Creek Formation (Montana), 75
Hill, Andrew, 82
hominin remains
DNA from, 81–82
Lucy, 83–84
tracks, 82, 83–84
Hominini, 81
Hominoidea, 80–81
*Homo erectus*, 84
*Homo habilis*, 84
*Homo sapiens*, 82
Hooke, Robert, 12–14
humans
Cambrian Explosion and, 57
chimpanzee relationship to, 80
coexistence of species of, 19–20, 20–21

evolution of, 78, 81–85, 87
information about evolution from fossils, 20–21
migrations out of Africa, 86–87, 88–89
modern behaviors of, 89–90
scientific family, 80–81
scientific "tribe," 81
Hutton, James, 38, 40

## I
Iceman, 23
*Iguanodon*, 19
imagination, 89–90
index fossils, 42–43

## J
Jefferson, Thomas, 18
Johanson, Donald, 82
Johnson, Kirk, 22–23, 71
*Jurassic West* (Foster), 75

## K
Kelvin, Lord (Baron Kelvin of Largs), 45, 46, 47
Kenya, 84
Kimeu, Kamoya, 84
KT boundary, 63–64

## L
La Brea Tar Pits, 27, 61, 77
Laborde, Albert, 45
lace crabs, 55
Laetoli site, 82
*Laggania*, 56
Lakes, Arthur, 60, 74
Leakey, Mary, 82
Leakey, Richard, 84
Lewis, Meriwether, 18
living fossils, 17
Lockley, Martin, 34
*Lord Kelvin and the Age of the Earth* (Burchfield), 46
Los Angeles, California, 27, 61, 77
*The Lost Dinosaurs of Egypt* (Nothdurft), 69
Lucas, O.W., 60
Lucy, 83–84
*Lucy, the Beginning of Humankind* (Johanson), 82
Lyell, Charles, 40–41

## M

macroscopic creatures, 43
mammal fossils, 74, 75
Mantell, Gideon, 17, 19
Mantell, Mary, 17, 19
*The Map That Changed the World* (Winchester), 41
Marsh, Othniel Charles, 60
*Masiakasaurus,* 76
Mason, Roger, 54
mass extinction events, 52, 63–64
mastodons, identifying, 8
Mayor, Adrienne, 10
McPhee, John, 38
*Megalonyx Jeffersoni,* 18
Mesozoic Era
   common name, 47
   dinosaurs during, 58–60
   evolution during, 58
   extinction at boundary with Paleozoic, 52, 64
meteors, evidence of impact, 63
Meyer, Herbert W., 27
microfossils, 43
*Micrographia* (Hooke), 12–14
microscopic life, 43, 47, 52
minerals, role of, 29–32
mitochondrial DNA, 88
mnemonic devices, example of, 49
molds, 32
Mongolia, 10–11
Morris, Simon Conway, 56
Morrison Formation (North America), 34, 58–59, 60, 71, 75
mudstone formations, 34, 71
mummification, natural
   described, 24–25
   of dinosaurs, 30–31, 75
myths, 8–9, 10

## N

"Nariokotome boy," 84
*National Geographic* (magazine), 34
natural selection, 17, 78, 87
Neander Valley, Germany, 81
Neandertals, 81, 87
Noah's floods, 9
Nothdurft, William, 69

## O

*Opabinia,* 57
*The Origin of Species* (Darwin), 17, 41, 78
original horizontality, principle of, 14
ossicles, 25
ostracods, 43
oxygen, 30, 52

## P

pachycephalsaurs, 75
Paleontological Research Institute (PRI), 67
paleontologists
   described, 7
   memory devices used by, 49
   recording and extracting methods used by, 72–74
   *See also specific individuals*
Paleozoic Era
   common name, 47
   evolution during, 55
   extinction at boundary with Mesozoic, 52, 64
   important fossil sites, 55–58
Parachute Creek Atlas Project, 63
*Paramylodon,* 25
Parker, Steve, 72
Permian Period, 52
permineralization, 29–32
petrification, 12, 28–32
Petrified Forest, Arizona, 28–30
*Peytoia,* 56, 57
Phanerozoic Eon, 47, 49
photosynthesis, 52
plants
   evolution of flowering, 58, 61
   Morrison Formation fossils of, 59
   orchids, 19
   of Paleozoic era, 55
   species-specific spores and pollen grains, 43
plastic forces of Earth, 12
Poinar, George, Jr., 25
Poinar, Roberta, 25
pond scum, 52
*The Practical Paleontologist* (Parker), 72
Precambrian Era, 52, 54
preservation
   in amber, 25

by carbonization, 27–28
low temperatures and, 23–24
by mummification, 24–25
in tar pits, 25, 27
principle of original horizontality, 14
principle of superposition, 14
*The Principles of Geology* (Lyell), 40
Proterozoic Era, 54
*Protoceratops,* 11
pseudomorphs, 32
*Psittacosaurus,* 11
Purgatoire River, Colorado, 34
pygmy race fossils, 19–20, 84–85

### R
radioactivity, 45–47
radium, 45–47
Rancho La Brea Tar Pits, 27, 61, 77
recordkeeping, 73
relative time, 43
replacement, 29–32
Rich, Thomas, 75
Rocky Mountains (U.S.), 61
Roman Catholic Church, 9, 14
Romans, ancient, 8, 9
Royal Saskatchewan Museum, Canada, 36
Rutherford, Ernest, 45–47
Rynie, Scotland, 55

### S
Sadiman (volcano), 83
sandstone formations, 34, 71
sauropods, 34, 59
search image development, 69
*The Seashell on the Mountaintop* (Cutler), 9
seashells, 12–14
sedimentary rocks, 47
sedimentation, 41
  *See also* deposition
sediments and water, 14
shale layers, 27
Shark Bay, Australia, 54
shells, 12–14, 32
Sloan, Christopher, 82–83
sloth skeletons, 25
Smith, William, 41–42
*Smithsonian Intimate Guide to Human Origins* (Sloan), 82–83
snakestones, 15

Sprigg, Reg, 54
Steno, Nicolaus, 9, 12, 14
Sternberg family, 30–31
Stewart, John, 18
strata and fossils, 41
stromatolites, 52, 54
superposition, principle of, 14
Sykes, Brian, 88

### T
*T. rex and the Crater of Doom* (Alvarez, Walter), 64
tar pits, 25, 27, 61
teeth, 12
temperatures, 23–24, 44–47
*Terrible Lizard* (Cadbury), 15
Tertiary Period, 52, 63
tetrapods, 55
*Theory of the Earth* (Hutton), 38
theropods, 34
Thompson, William, 45, 46, 47
time
  absolute scale for, 44
  geological divisions, 47, 50–51
  index fossils as markers of relative, 43
Toba eruption, 89
tongue stones, 12
trace fossils, 33–34
tracks
  casts of, 34
  dinosaur, 34, 36, 71
  hominin, 82, 83–84
Triassic Period, 52
*Triceratops,* 36
trilobites
  evolution of, 55
  as index fossils, 43
  molds of, 32–33
Troll, Ray, 71
*Tyrannosaurus rex,* 36
Tyson, Edward, 80

### U
*Under a Green Sky* (Ward), 64
Uniformitarianism, 40–41
United States Geological Service (USGS), 43, 67
United States Geological Surveys, 18
uplift, 40, 41
uranium, 45, 46–47

## V

Venezuela, 78
vestigial organs, 80

## W

Walcott, Charles Doolittle, 55–56, 58
Ward, Peter, 64, 65
Wells, Spencer, 88
Western Interior Paleontological Association (WIPS), 67
White, Tim, 82
Whittington, H.G., 56–57
Winchester, Simon, 41
*Wonderful Life* (Gould), 57

# About the Author

▲

Award-winning author and illustrator **GARY RAHAM** has written more than a dozen books of either science fact or science fiction for adults and children and hundreds of nature articles for the general public. He has contributed to *Highlights for Children*, *Cricket*, and Discovery Channel Books. Teachers use Raham's science-fiction book *The Deep Time Diaries* as a way to teach both science fact and the techniques of creative fiction. A former science teacher, Raham also contributes to the science of paleontology by working with a volunteer organization called the Western Interior Paleontological Society (WIPS). See some of his work at www.biostration.com.